...RD, NJ 08084

And Tyler, Too? Stratford Public Library
A Fict

Massey,   3 8092 00006 6962

AND TYLER, TOO?

AND TYLER, TOO?

•

Ellen Gray Massey

AVALON BOOKS
THOMAS BOUREGY AND COMPANY, INC.
401 LAFAYETTE STREET
NEW YORK, NEW YORK 10003

© Copyright 1998 by Ellen Gray Massey
Library of Congress Catalog Card Number 98-96069
ISBN 0-8034-9295-2
All rights reserved.
All the characters in this book are fictitious,
and any resemblance to actual persons,
living or dead, is purely coincidental.

PRINTED IN THE UNITED STATES OF AMERICA
ON ACID-FREE PAPER
BY HADDON CRAFTSMEN, BLOOMSBURG, PENNSYLVANIA

For Frances and John
A bit of New York City, Portugal, and the Missouri Ozarks

Chapter One

Her parents and the black-haired artist never took their eyes off of Willow. Though visible from the fifteenth-story window, the view and the activity in the street below Macy's Department Store were ignored. Willow Hill was studying one at a time the designs and motifs piled neatly on the table in front of her. Her dark, carefully made-up eyebrows lowered in concentration as she quickly discarded most of the sheets of art paper, but a few she examined carefully before laying them to one side.

"Nice, don't you think, Paula?" she said to her designer as she paused at a red-and-yellow design involving a clown. Paula nodded enthusiastically.

The concentrated expression on the artist's face did not change, but the middle-aged couple beamed as they watched their youngest child at work.

Willow traced a well-manicured finger around the clown. "He has a unique look—typical clown, but still an individual," she said. "And this bold background swirl. I like it, don't you?" She didn't look up to see Paula's silent approval. "Just what we need for our new spring line of related separates."

"Just exactly," Paula agreed.

Willow continued, "That roguish look in the clown's eyes should appeal to little boys. I can see my nephew liking it." Together they discussed how to use that design before putting the sheet on top of the pile of those she might purchase. Without looking up, she picked up the next design, an allover black-and-white pattern, which she quickly discarded before selecting a pastel that pleased her.

With businesslike efficiency, Willow paid no attention to the three spectators in the small design room of Mansfield & Logan, Inc., manufacturers of quality children's clothing. To her left, seated on folding chairs squeezed together temporarily into the space not taken up by the big table where Willow was working, were her visiting parents and the artist, a medium-sized young man in his late twenties.

Not once during the fifteen minutes that had passed since she started studying the designs did Willow look up, though Paula smiled at Willow's parents and sneaked frequent glances at the handsome artist and back at Willow. He didn't notice her attentions because he never took his eyes from Willow.

Watching her daughter look at pieces of art paper for a quarter of an hour was enough inactivity for Maggie Hill. When she had seen all she wanted of the view out the window that overlooked the city, her attention turned to the young man. He was much more interesting. She noted how intently he was watching Willow and detected his greater interest in her daughter than in some possible sales. She touched her husband's leg to get his attention and, by rolling her eyes and cocking her head, silently asked him to notice the artist.

And Tyler, Too?

Jerry studied him briefly, raised his right eyebrow in surprise, glanced quickly at Willow, and then back to the artist. Grinning, he winked at his wife and nodded.

Unable to remain silent any longer, in a half whisper that didn't disturb her daughter, Maggie asked the young man, "Does she always ignore you like this?"

The artist took his eyes from Willow and turned to Maggie. His impish grin lit up his serious face, making his neat black mustache dance on his lip. "Always," he said, and laughed.

Maggie and Jerry exchanged glances of amazement. Maggie shook her head while Jerry lifted his hands and screwed up his face in amazement at their daughter's blindness. Here was a talented, handsome, and delightful man. Well, they had to admit, his clothes were rather strange to their conservative views—stark black shirt, jacket, vest, and pants, all loose and layered, with silver jewelry. But they saw no harm in that. He was an artist, wasn't he? Just added to his charm. And their unmarried daughter ignored him!

"Have you known her long . . . uh, Mr. Tyler, isn't it?" Jerry asked. Willow had introduced them quickly when he entered unexpectedly with his portfolio of designs. Willow had been showing her parents around her office on their first trip to visit her as head fashion merchandiser of the New York manufacturing firm. When Tyler showed up, she welcomed the opportunity to let her parents witness her in action. In spite of her success in the big city, they still treated her as a kid. Willow could not resist showing off how well a Midwestern, small-town girl fit into the exciting garment industry scene of New York City.

"Yes, Hugh Tyler," the artist repeated his name, and handed Jerry his business card. "My friends just call me Tyler. And yes, I've known her for about three years." At the surprised reaction of the couple, he added, "But unfortunately only professionally. Mansfield and Logan is one of my clients. Since Willow has been with them, they buy from twenty to twenty-five of my designs each year."

"That's good, isn't it?" Maggie asked.

"Yes, very good. More than any other client. Today isn't my regular run. I had some new designs that I thought she might be able to use. I just dropped in. I do that sometimes when I need some extra money," he said, and grinned. "And I can always count on her buying a few pieces."

"Seems like a good arrangement," Jerry said.

"Yes, it is. A good business arrangement."

Though Tyler was speaking to them, he kept glancing back at Willow. She was leaning over another design, half rising from her chair to view it better. Her bracelets clinked on the table as she pointed out details that pleased her, while her dangling earrings swayed against her white throat. Her carefully coiffured, blue-black head was close to Paula's blond one as they discussed the possibilities of the marine design before them.

"How do you like living in the city?" Maggie asked Tyler.

"Huh? Oh, fine. I'm used to it."

"This is our first trip here," she said. "I don't like it."

"People here aren't friendly enough for her," Jerry said, winking at Maggie. "They look at her like she's

And Tyler, Too?

going to rob them or something when she tries to start a conversation."

"Oh, Jerry, they do not," Maggie said, and slapped him playfully on the leg. "This young man doesn't act that way."

"Well, he knows you're Willow's mother. He has to act nice so she'll buy his stuff." Jerry laughed to show he was joking.

Ignoring her husband, Maggie asked, "Were you born in New York, Hugh?"

"Oh no, hardly. Portugal."

"Oh!" Maggie said. "But your name doesn't sound..."

Tyler laughed. "Americanized it. A better name to sell my artwork."

The Hills gave each other a worried look. "Then you're just here temporarily?" Maggie asked.

"Oh no." His boyish grin deepened the small cleft in his chin. As he shook his head, his longish hair rubbed across his collar and the sculptured silver pendant on his leather thong necklace swung against the zipper of his jacket, making a slight jingle. "My parents moved here when I was small. I don't go back there anymore, but someday, maybe not until I retire, but someday, I'd like to get out of this city into the open country."

The Hills smiled at each other. Jerry raised his right eyebrow and again winked at Maggie.

After Maggie got the conversation started, Tyler was quite talkative, asking questions himself. "You're from Missouri, I understand?"

"Yes, a small town nobody much ever heard of in the Ozarks," Jerry said proudly.

"You're lucky."

"Yes, we think so, too," Maggie said. "We know that to succeed in the fashion world, New York is the place to be, and we are resigned to Willow being here...."

"But we don't understand," Jerry finished for her, "with her raising, how she can be happy here all by herself. We know she misses the family and the rivers and trees and hills at home."

They pondered that enigma in silence for a few minutes while they watched Willow. Though aware that they were talking about her, Willow was too engrossed in her work to pay much attention to their conversation. She knew her mother could get anyone to talking. She heard only bits and pieces of the conversation as she and Paula studied and conferred over Tyler's designs and how they could use them. Willow wasn't consciously aware that she was trying to find uses for as many of his designs as she could.

In a softer tone than before, Maggie asked Tyler, "Why don't you and your wife come to the Ozarks on your vacation and see for yourself how nice it is?"

Tyler laughed, looked at her, and then quickly glanced again at Willow. "I'm not married. Never have been."

"I didn't think so," Maggie said with mischief in her eyes. "I didn't think that big silver ring on your finger was a wedding ring. Just checking."

Tyler grinned. He knew what she was up to and was enjoying the attention he was getting. "And, Mrs. Hill, I'll answer your next question before you ask it. Yes, I do like your daughter, but she won't let me get any closer to her than this." He pointed to the big table separating them and with his hands indicated a wall between them.

"Pity," Jerry said.

Tyler nodded, his chin cleft deepening.

"Then come to our family gathering next month," Maggie said in a louder voice than she intended.

Just then Willow looked up from the last design. "Mother!" Her normally rosy, round face deepened in color, and she slumped slightly in her chair in despair at this mother of hers. She was no longer the efficient young executive, but an embarrassed daughter rebelling against her mother's interference. "Mom, this is New York. You don't go around inviting just anyone off the streets into your home."

"She was just being friendly," Jerry said in support of his wife, surprised at Willow's angry tone. He patted Maggie's hand that it was all right. Her daughter's chastisement didn't faze Maggie. She smiled. At least she had forced Willow to notice this young man.

"Oh, I know," Willow said. Then noticing the hurt in Tyler's eyes because she'd referred to him as "just anyone off the streets," she looked straight at him for the first time and said, "I'm sorry, Tyler. I didn't mean that the way it sounded."

"That's okay, I understand."

"You'll have to excuse my mother."

"Nothing to excuse. I had a mother who never stopped practicing old-fashioned hospitality. Besides, I've enjoyed visiting with your parents." Tyler smiled at Maggie to show her he appreciated her invitation. His gracious manner put everyone at ease.

Once again the businesswoman, Willow concluded her transactions. Tyler wrote out an invoice for the three designs she wanted. On her way out of the room with the designs and her papers, she turned back to Tyler. He had risen from his chair as soon as she did. "Tyler, you'll bring me more designs when you have them?" she asked pleasantly. "These today were especially good."

"Should have some more in a few weeks." Tyler held the door for her. In the narrow passageway to the door, Willow accidentally bumped against him, dropping some of her papers. Tyler quickly collected them for her.

Maggie and Jerry exchanged looks that questioned how their daughter could resist his engaging smile and charming manners.

"Good," Willow said. "I'll be looking forward to seeing them. We'll be needing some summer designs. Maybe some more clowns. And animals are always good."

"I've got some ideas," Tyler said.

"Fine. Have a nice summer," she said politely. She started out, but turned back to say, "Tyler, in just four weeks I'm off to the Ozarks. Swimming in the river, canoeing, hiking, eating my mother's cooking, playing with my niece and nephew! I can't wait." Her happy smile obliterated her former aloofness. Her blue eyes framed by long black lashes seemed to already see her home and family instead of the artist before her.

"Enjoy yourself," Tyler barely had time to say before she spun around rapidly on her stylish heels, and, her full skirt swishing gracefully from her hips, walked down the hall. His pleased smile was still on his face when he turned to say good-bye to Maggie and Jerry.

And Tyler, Too?

"I can see that she doesn't give you much of a chance," Jerry said.

"Not much," Tyler agreed. "That's the longest conversation we've ever had that didn't include business." He walked to the table to gather up his designs and arranged them carefully in special slots in his two carrying cases. When he had everything gathered and his cases strapped on his luggage cart, he said, "I enjoyed meeting and talking with you both. Usually I just sit in here quietly while your daughter scrutinizes my work."

He looked down to the end of the empty hall to the open door of Willow's office where, while giving Paula instructions, Willow kept glancing back at them. "I sometimes envy my designs because they come under those determined eyes of hers. If I were one of my designs, then at least she might notice me." He laughed self-consciously because he had revealed more to these strangers than he intended.

"She's a one-track sort of person. When she's working on something, everything else gets pushed aside," Maggie said.

"And now her consuming project is her career," Jerry said.

Tyler nodded. "Don't I know." He looked down the hall at Willow, who was busily explaining to Paula the use she intended for the new designs. Paula was nodding enthusiastically. Though ostensibly concentrating on the work, Willow was aware that Tyler was still there talking to her parents.

"You've got quite a daughter," Tyler said.

"Yes, we know," Maggie said.

Jerry agreed. "Right after graduating from college,

she loaded up her old car with all it could carry and drove all by herself to New York City to look for a job.''

"Yes," Maggie said proudly. "And in just a few years she's now head of a department." Maggie scanned the room and the view out the window of the skyscraper. She shook her head. "I see it, but I don't believe it. She is still my little girl. She hates it when I say that, so I don't anymore in her presence."

Tyler seemed to understand how mothers were. He smiled in sympathy.

As Jerry shook Tyler's hand in parting, he handed Tyler a crumpled slip of paper. "My wife's invitation was real," he said. "We'd love to have you join us."

Surprised, Tyler opened the paper, but before he could read it, Jerry added, "Our address and phone number and the dates of the family shindig next month to welcome Willow home. Come for the float trip, June eighteenth and nineteenth."

Surprised and pleased, Tyler grinned, his black eyes alive with pleasure. "That'd be something, all right. I've never been to the Ozarks. I hear it's a great place."

"That it is, my boy, that it is," Jerry said.

"Do come." Maggie laid her hand on his arm to encourage him. "It's lots of fun floating down the river. We'll be in touch."

Chapter Two

Willow Hill had been upset ever since Hugh Tyler had showed up yesterday afternoon at her family gathering in Missouri. A complete surprise to her, though she soon learned that everyone else was expecting him. Though her family meant more to her than anything in the world except her job in New York City, she hated their continual prying into her love life, their introducing her to possible boyfriends, and their continually making comments such as, "Who's the latest prospect for becoming Mr. Willow Hill?"

After her brother Charley first said this, it became a favorite of her family, always followed by good-natured laughing and meaningful pokes. Okay, so she was independent, and, she admitted, a take-charge person who had no time for socializing. That was her business. She had tolerated her family's interference because she knew they did it out of love for her.

But this time her parents had gone too far in inviting, of all people, Tyler, a suave, urban sophisticate. Her parents' brief meeting with him a month ago in New York surely showed them how different he was from all the other guys they had foisted off on her over the years. His long hair, his jewelry, his offbeat clothing. His precarious living as an artist. Surely they saw that he was not a man they could admire. What possessed them to invite him?

Of course she knew he was interested in her. She'd have been blind not to notice how he looked at her each time he brought in his designs, but she had kept him at a distance. Could it be that she was more conservative than her parents? His artistic temperament and modern big-city conduct was the opposite of the small-town heritage she still clung to, even though she would probably always work and live in New York.

In spite of her annoyance, she realized that she was the one who was narrow-minded. She couldn't help it. Tyler's presence was spoiling this canoe trip that she had anticipated all year while cooped up in her skyscraper.

Even more mysterious than why her parents could think of including such an outsider was that he actually accepted. He had nothing in common with her two brothers, one a CPA and the other a businessman in a small town. Or with her cousin Mitch, an auctioneer. And what a difference in the landscape! The sycamores and maples bordering the wild river were nothing like the tall, steel buildings walling in New York's streets. The silent blue heron standing in the shallow water and the row of turtles sunning themselves on a log downstream bore no resemblance to the never-ending flow of noisy humanity on the city streets where Tyler was raised.

She conceded, however, that Hugh Tyler here in Missouri was different from the man she knew only in a professional way in the city. As soon as he arrived, minus his ostentatious silver jewelry and

And Tyler, Too?

dressed in jeans and T-shirt like everyone else, he fit right into the activities of her family. Her small niece and nephew adored him, following him every place he went.

Making the best of a bad situation, she reasoned that she could shake him on the float trip. When cars of those who planned to take the overnight float drove down the narrow country road to the gravel bar where they would put in, Willow was eager to pick out the canoe that she and her cousin Mitch would take. But having arrived earlier in his big truck with the four canoes and their gear, Mitch and her father had other plans.

"Willow." Her father beckoned her to the last canoe pulled onto the narrow end of the gravel bar. Only the bow of the canoe rested on the gravel. The back was floating in four feet of water. Already seated in the back, with a paddle in his hand and a big grin on his attractive face, was the artist. "This is your canoe, Willow," Jerry said.

A quick glance told her that her brothers and their wives were climbing into the two other canoes, and Mitch was already pushing his canoe into the stream. Mitch jumped in and waved to Willow. "Race you to the first riffle," he dared her.

To begin every float, the Hill family started off with a race to see which canoe would be the first to enter the narrow, fast water of the riffle, which was about a quarter of a mile downstream at the end of the long eddy. The eddies on this river ranged from four to ten feet deep and from a quarter of a mile to two miles in length. Ever since they were old enough to handle a canoe by themselves, Willow and Mitch had teamed together, competing with the others. And usually winning. But by the time she reached the water's edge, Mitch and his wife, Amy, were already in midstream back-paddling to stay in place, waiting for her. They both grinned with the success of their strategy in pairing Willow with Hugh Tyler.

She had no choice but to make the float with Tyler. "Okay, you guys," she yelled at them. "But I'm in the back." Her tone told the others that no greenhorn would guide her canoe. Shocked by her rude manner, her father started to object, but Tyler quickly avoided any further discussion.

"Sure," he said, and holding to the gunnels, crawled to the front of the unsteady canoe, sat down, and held out his hand to help Willow climb in. Though she didn't need his assistance, she allowed him to help her. With experienced grace, she moved to the back. While she was picking up the paddle from the bottom of the canoe and turning around to sit down, her niece and nephew plunged into the shallow water beside the canoe.

"We're going with you, Aunt Willow," Cory said, pushing aside his cousin to climb in first.

"Yeah," five-year-old Dawn yelled, splashing into the water which was almost waist-high to her. "Wait for me!" Dawn grabbed the gunnel. She pulled the canoe from its precarious perch on the gravel just as her collie leaped into the canoe behind Tyler.

"Wait a minute, guys," Willow shouted, grabbing the gunnels as the canoe rocked. Scrambling to climb in, the children tipped the boat. Still facing the back, Willow didn't have time to turn around or use the paddle to control the canoe. Dawn's final heave to get

And Tyler, Too?

inside threw Willow off balance. The canoe overturned, dunking the children, Tyler, Willow, and the dog into the warm, clear water.

Screaming with delight at their adventure, and held up by their orange life jackets, the children bobbed downstream with the slow current. The collie, with only his head above water, paddled in a circle to see where everyone was before heading for the shore. In the shallow water, Tyler quickly regained his feet, grabbed the canoe, and pulled its nose back onto the gravel bar. Willow made the biggest splash. With arms and legs sprawling, her thin body disappeared in a spray of river water.

After the momentary surprise, everyone laughed, enjoying the show. The couples in the other canoes and Willow's parents on the gravel bar made no effort at rescue, for the water was not deep. When Willow's feet found the rocky bottom of the river so she could stand up, she was only shoulder-deep in water.

"Hi, Tippy," her brother Gene teased her. She laughed good-naturedly. She knew she deserved the name, given by family tradition to the first one to upset a canoe on each float. She'd be "Tippy," short for Tippecanoe, for the rest of the trip.

Mitch, a history buff, was familiar with the 1839 presidential campaign slogan of William Henry Harrison, hero of the Battle of Tippecanoe, and his vice-presidential candidate, John Tyler. Mitch laughed more than the others at the coincidence of the names.

"Tippecanoe!" He paddled his canoe up to Willow, having trouble containing his mirth. "And Tyler, too," he added with a knowing look at Hugh Tyler, whose varicolored T-shirt and denim cutoffs were dripping.

Willow's parents glanced at each other almost as if Tyler's name itself was justification enough for their invitation. "Isn't that perfect?" Maggie Hill said.

Her husband nodded.

Tyler's broad grin lit up his face. The coincidence appealed to him. Willow relaxed. She knew she could not win against her entire family. She laughed along with the others, enjoying this joke.

After their fun, those in the canoes picked up the floating children. Cory complained when Mitch started to put them in his canoe. "No, we want to go with Hugh and Aunt Willow."

"No, kids, not today," Mitch said, interpreting a gesture from Maggie to leave Willow and Tyler alone.

"That's okay," Willow said, knowing what everyone was trying to do. She hoped her relatives' actions were not as obvious to Tyler. "I'd love to have them." She really meant it. The children's presence would keep the trip with Tyler from being a complete washout. She came home to be with her family, not with a piece of the city. "C'mon, kids."

She grabbed each floating child by the life jacket straps and waded to the shore, dragging them with her.

"You got all wet, Aunt Willow." Dawn laughed at her aunt's short, black hair plastered to her head like a tight cap.

"So did you, pumpkin," she said, splashing more water at her.

The children reciprocated, using both hands and feet to spray her. "I'll get you," she said as she dragged them to where their feet could touch bottom.

And Tyler, Too?

This time Jerry held the canoe steady until Willow, the children, and Tyler were settled in. The collie ran back and forth on the gravel bar, ready to leap in. Maggie caught him and held him firmly. The dog gave one sorrowful bark and strained against his collar.

"Can Barney come, Aunt Willow?" Dawn asked, biting her lower lip.

"Sure, why not? The more the merrier." Barney was a seasoned canoeist, having been on many floats.

The moment Maggie let him go, Barney jumped into the canoe to his usual place behind the front paddler and immediately shook the river water from him. Seated side by side on Styrofoam pads in the middle, the children whooped at the unexpected shower.

"Off you go." Jerry shoved the canoe into the current, the aluminum bottom scraping noisily on the loose gravel.

"Anchors aweigh!" Tyler sang, brandishing his paddle as the canoe floated backward. Expertly, with one sweep of her paddle, Willow pointed the nose downstream to follow the other three canoes that were already disappearing around the bend. Mitch and her brothers were vying to reach the riffle first. She waved to her parents, still on the gravel bar.

"See you tonight at the gravel bar at Fall-in-Bluff Eddy," Jerry called. This time he and Maggie elected to forgo the float in order to help with the logistics of getting the group on and off the river and meeting them at night to avoid taking the tents and heavy camping equipment in the canoes.

"Have a good time," Maggie called.

A quick glance back, before Willow had to give her total attention to guiding the canoe, showed her parents grinning and waving with arms around each other. Willow groaned. She looked ahead at Tyler seated in the front with a rapt expression on his face as he surveyed the river scene around him. *Oh, well, they mean well,* she thought, just as her canoe entered the first rocky riffle.

As they were carried more rapidly in the quickened current through the narrow passage, Tyler tentatively thrust out his paddle to help. Behind him stood the collie with his legs apart for balance, ready to leap out if necessary.

"Don't paddle unless I tell you," Willow said. Obviously Tyler knew very little about canoeing. As the swift current bore the canoe directly toward a half-submerged log on their left, she said, "Now! Paddle hard on your left."

While Willow was busy controlling the canoe with her paddle from the back, Tyler gave several powerful thrusts with his paddle, turning the canoe away from the danger.

"Now on the right!" Willow yelled. Just beyond the log, the river turned abruptly left. Two thrusts by Tyler, plus a shove with his paddle against a tree trunk, helped the canoe out of the narrow, winding passageway into a calm, open eddy of water.

Lazily floating down the eddy ahead of them was Mitch's canoe. He had held back to be sure the last canoe came through the riffle. The delighted screams of the children, followed by Willow's thumbs-up sign, told him they were okay, even with an inexperienced front man. "Right on!" Mitch yelled and paddled to catch up to the others.

Willow was impressed with Tyler. She'd taught sev-

And Tyler, Too?

eral people to be her front paddler, though none had caught on as quickly. The natural reaction when the canoe is about to hit something is to paddle on the opposite side—which action, any canoeist knows, will force the craft straight into the object. Tyler did exactly what she told him to do, instantly understanding the reason. Because of his artistic sense of space, she reasoned. She looked at him with new respect, though all she could see over the children's heads and the collie was his broad back and wet black hair.

"Outstanding!" Tyler said, turning half around to see the whitecapped water spilling from the riffle they just rode. The wild rushing water in the background framed Willow. Her sloppy shirt and shorts still dripping water and hair still plastered to her forehead, she glided as one with her canoe. In the calm water, her paddle lay carelessly across her bare knees.

"You done good!" Willow laughed when she caught his eyes on her.

"I've never experienced anything like it. Incredible!"

The children were happily chatting and dangling their hands over the sides. With an almost unnoticed motion with her paddle every so often, Willow kept the canoe in the slow current in the center of the river.

Now that there was no need for him to paddle, Tyler resumed his examination of the river. He showed the children a muskrat swimming along the bank.

The quiet river carrying them lazily downstream soon dispelled Willow's bad mood, as it had always done for her when she was growing up. The river was her solace. And she admitted to herself that she may have overreacted. Though she was still disappointed not to be with Mitch, Tyler's presence was not a disaster. The children, as well as everyone else in the family since his arrival yesterday, were enjoying his company.

She was on the river with her family, but isolated with Tyler, just the same. Mitch and her brothers ahead seemed to be in a plot to keep some distance away. Willow didn't paddle to catch up, for she so enjoyed being on the river again that she chose the lazy pace.

"My family!" She sighed aloud with resigned amusement. "What they won't do."

"I think they are great." Tyler turned to face her with his charming smile. "I don't have any family over here." They heard the cheerful call of the meadowlark. A blue heron half hidden in the backwaters of a cove watched them pass.

"And my whole family is here," Willow said.

"Last month in the city, while your parents were visiting in your office, did you know what they were up to when I came in with my designs?"

Willow nodded. "Yes. I knew from their actions soon after you walked in. Up to their old tricks to fix me up. I've learned a long time ago to ignore them. But I certainly never expected you to take them seriously."

Tyler gestured with his arm to indicate the river view and the children before concentrating on her. "Why wouldn't I? They were serious about the invitation. And for me, an adventure in a scenic place, with a close family and . . ." He looked admiringly at her. ". . . a beautiful woman. I couldn't resist."

"I never expected you—"

And Tyler, Too? 21

"Ah." He shook his head slightly. "You don't know enough about me to 'expect' anything." He cocked his head and raised his eyebrows to dare her to deny that.

He was right. She knew nothing about him outside of his remarkable artistic ability. But she was quickly learning. The past few hours had proved that he was not the stereotyped New Yorker she had pegged him, though he didn't have to tell her that he had no family here in this area. She already assumed that.

"Aunt Willow, when can we go swimming?" Cory asked.

Glad of his interruption, Willow said, "Soon." Then to Tyler, "There's a great place just down the river." To cover her embarrassment and to get there sooner, Willow started paddling with slow, steady strokes. The canoe slid noiselessly through the water.

She shook her head wondering why she kept letting herself get manipulated like this. Surely back in her office she should have foreseen what her parents were up to when they conferred so long with Tyler. Recalling the bits of conversations she heard, she realized that she did know what her parents were planning. What surprised her was Tyler's acceptance. Coming all the way to Missouri on a casual invitation!

Tyler was right. She didn't know him at all. But then she didn't want to know him. She was still irritable that he ruined her day with Mitch. At least she could enjoy the kids.

"You can jump off the rope this time. You're both big enough," she said to the children.

They both clapped their hands in glee. Barney's tail slapped back and forth against the aluminum boat as if he too would join in their fun.

Chapter Three

"Aunt Willow," Cory said. He had crawled back into the canoe to her and raised up his freckled face a foot from hers. Even the rocking of the canoe hadn't broken her concentration on the rerun of the scene in her office. "Aunt Willow, aren't we ever going swimming?"

"Of course. Just around the bend."

Since he didn't need to help with the paddling, Tyler had pulled his pad and pencils out of his backpack. He was rapidly sketching. Barney's head was hanging over one shoulder and Dawn the other.

"You draw good," Dawn said.

In response, he glanced at her and sketched her face. He added her dimple to her cheek.

"Me, too," Cory said.

With a few dexterous strokes, Tyler drew the boy's head, tore the sheets from his pad, and gave them to the children. Thrilled, they showed them to Willow.

Though she was quite familiar with his overall fabric designs and the juvenile motifs that she purchased from him to use on children's clothing, she had not seen his portrait work. She could hardly take her eyes off of them to give them back to the children. In a

And Tyler, Too?

few lines he had caught Cory's impulsiveness and Dawn's sensitivity.

"These are great, Tyler. I didn't know that you . . ." Then she remembered his reminding her she really knew nothing about him. She truly did not.

Tyler smiled, more pleased at her compliment here of these hurried sketches than he was in her office, as she was paying good prices for his finished designs. "I used to do that at the mall to make enough money to live on when I couldn't sell my serious stuff," he said.

They couldn't say more, for they needed their concentration for the riffle. Tyler bent low as they floated under an overhanging sycamore. "Heads down," he called to the children. Dawn grabbed Barney and held him down as they glided harmlessly under the branches. Broad leaves tickled their heads. Cory brushed away the spider's web that streamed back from Tyler. Without being told, Tyler used his paddle both as a pole and an oar to help turn the tight corner and avoid the big boulders in the path of the choppy current.

"Submerged rock on the right," Tyler called out. He had learned to recognize the hidden obstacles by the change in the water flow. Using her paddle as a rudder and back-paddling, Willow forced the canoe to the left around the boulders out of the fastest flow into the quieter water under the tree branches. She changed directions too late to miss the boulder completely. With a loud metallic clank, the canoe bottom scraped and bumped over the corner of the submerged rock, tilting the canoe to the left.

"Hold tight!" Willow called over the squeals of the

children as they grabbed the crossbar in front of them to keep from falling against the left side of the canoe. Willow pushed the canoe away from the rock with her paddle. Her motion and the swirl of water from the boulder sent them broadside against the mudbank. Both Willow and Tyler fought to straighten the canoe. Tyler paddled savagely to avoid the bank. Willow managed to point the canoe downstream just before they entered a tight bend.

There were whitecaps on the tops of the waves as the total flow of the river spilled into the new bend. Looking ahead to find the point of the vee, where the water congregated to get through the narrow outlet and the ideal place to ride the riffle, Willow made several backstrokes. Tyler put his paddle out into the water as far as he could reach on his right and pulled into the canoe to bring the bow into the main current. Together they straightened the canoe, heading perfectly into the swift water between a half-submerged log on one side and the weed-covered gravel bar on the other.

When the canoe was headed in the correct direction, the current took them through with Willow making only short strokes to hold them in the current away from the rocks. Though it didn't rate as rapids, the fall of the land made this riffle the fastest one so far.

"Whooo-eeee!" Tyler yelled when they turned the last bend and he saw ahead the calm expanse of the next eddy. Though she had floated the river many times, Willow never lost her delight. Experiencing it with a newcomer and through the eyes of the children was like being here for the first time herself. She noticed details she would have overlooked had she and Mitch been together.

And Tyler, Too?

For instance, she never paid much attention to the contrasts—the wildness of the narrow riffle and the peace of the open eddy. Sunlight reflected in ragged, rippling streaks toward them across the blue-green surface. Every shade of green on Tyler's palette of paints in the trees, bushes, and vines crowding the edge of the water seemed to be protecting the calm eddy. There were trees leaning far out over the water. In the distance at the end of the long eddy, blue hills overlapped one another. Light clouds speckled the bright blue sky.

However, the scene that excited the children was the sight of the other three canoes pulled up onto the gravel bar near the end of the eddy. Their parents and cousin Mitch were putting out lunch.

"This is the Dawson Eddy," Willow told Tyler. "We always stop here. It's sort of ours." To the left was the broad gravel bar ringed with willow trees. On the right was the bluff where the river made a bend as it narrowed into a rocky riffle ahead.

"What do you mean, ours?"

"Our land along here." Willow pointed to her right with her paddle.

"Hi, Tippy," Mitch called as Willow's canoe joined them. "Come join us. And Tyler, too." He laughed. "How about a swim and lunch?" he asked the children.

Barney jumped out before the nose of the canoe scraped the gravel, and the children, handing their drawings to Willow for safekeeping, tumbled out right behind him. With squeals of delight, children and collie splashed in the sparkling water.

Mitch pulled the canoe onto the bar. "I'll beat you

to that sycamore over there," he said, pointing diagonally across the river where a white tree trunk leaned far out over the water. From its branches hung a solitary rope with knots tied in it.

"You're on," Willow said, stashing the drawings into a plastic bag and making a shallow dive into the deeper water. Everyone watched the contest. Mitch reached the rope first, and climbing it hand over hand and holding his legs up out of the water, swung it slightly and dropped back into the river, making as big a splash as he could. Willow swam on until she could swing herself up onto the sycamore trunk. She ignored the spray from his splash, but walked the trunk to the bank and climbed the boards tacked to a maple tree up to a big fork in its trunk.

"I beat you," she taunted Mitch.

Laughing, he tossed her the end of the rope. Holding on as high as she could reach, she swung out into the air, dropping beside Mitch, who was treading water. They both went under, coming up laughing and wrestling in fun.

The children were begging their parents to let them join Willow and Mitch. "Willow said we could," Cory said. Since the children wore life jackets and the current here was barely perceptible, the parents agreed when Willow nodded that she did promise them. Each child grabbed Tyler by a hand and pulled him into the river after them. They were soon floating, though Tyler could wade except in the deep water in the center of the river.

Cory and Dawn took turns swinging out and dropping from the rope. Willow was in the river to retrieve the children when they fell into the water, while Mitch stayed in the maple to ensure they had a tight hold before he gave them a push to swing them out over the river.

"C'mon, Tyler," the children yelled. "You do it."

Tyler was content to float lazily in the water near Willow as he watched the others. "This is sure different from the ocean," he said.

"Great, isn't it?" she asked. Her attention was on the children.

He looked at her in his own particular manner, which Willow was beginning to recognize. Probably he had always looked this way, but she hadn't noticed before. Holding his head bent slightly down, he looked up at her. His dark eyes, peering from under his raised eyebrows, seemed always to be full of wonder. Always studying and analyzing.

"I've never experienced anything like it," he said. "It's like a story, Huck Finn and Tom Sawyer. Did you realize that this whole morning we haven't seen anyone but us?"

"Sure. We rarely do on this stretch. That's one reason why we like it. On some of the other rivers we'd have to share the river with other groups. Also, this is a good stretch for kids, not too deep. Only in the middle of some of the eddies is it too deep for adults to wade."

Cory splashed down beside Tyler. This time the boy wouldn't be put off with any excuses. Tyler had to jump with him. As Tyler climbed up the boards right behind Cory, Mitch was swinging out into the river. He held on to the rope as it swung back toward the tree, and with his feet against the trunk, gave a powerful push that sent him far out into the river before he let go.

"Last time, Cory," he said as he tossed the rope up to Tyler. "Your mom has lunch ready." He waded to the gravel bar and patted Barney, who had been swimming the river to try to keep up with the children.

"Daddy and Mitch nailed these boards here," Cory explained as he scrambled up the tree trunk. "We come here lots to swim." When Tyler was beside him in the tree fork, he asked the boy, "Is there a way to get here besides down the river?"

"Yeah." Cory pointed behind him away from the river toward the field. "That's Grammy and Gramps's farm."

Tyler looked with great interest across the river bottom fields of hay, corn, and soybeans. Then he turned to Willow, who was on the bank below them ready to climb up the ladder for her turn. "Is that where you grew up?" he asked her.

"Partly. We moved to town when I was ten. The farm is rented out now."

"Beautiful." Though the valley was narrower at this point on the river because of the ridge and bluff behind it, he could see the house and other farm buildings about a quarter of a mile away.

"Daddy brings me down here lots of times," Cory said, touching Tyler's arm to get his attention. "We swim and fish. And sometimes we hike up that old trail over there to Grandma Edna's cabin." He pointed away from the main buildings to a spot closer to them. Up on the ridge of the bluff overlooking the river was a small log house, almost hidden in the encroaching trees. However, partway up the slope of the hill to the

And Tyler, Too?

top of the bluff, there was an open trail from the farm buildings to the lonely cabin.

Tyler cocked his head toward Willow, asking for more details.

"Grandma Edna Dawson is a several times great-grandmother who lived there. We sometimes have family outings at her cabin. We make sort of an excursion of it to repair the cabin, or at least keep it from falling down."

"Oh, and keep the road cleared?"

"No, we don't have to. Nature takes care of that. The trail goes over an area where there is no soil, only rocks. Trees can't grow. It's an Ozark glade with huge stone slabs on the surface."

Tired of this conversation, Cory pulled on Tyler's cutoffs. "Let's jump."

"Ladies first," Willow said. She grabbed on to the rope just above a knot and swung out. She dropped and tossed the rope back to Tyler.

"Okay, Cory. Your turn."

"I want to jump with Tyler, too." He frowned when everyone laughed. Almost ready to cry because of the teasing he didn't understand, he turned to Tyler.

"That's okay, buddy." Tyler grabbed him up in a bear hug and, taking a firm hold on the rope, swung out from the tree together. "They're just making fun of my name." They splashed down beside Willow, knocking her feet out from under her.

"Lunch is ready," Cory's mother called when the splashing and laughing quieted enough for them to hear her.

After lunch Tyler asked so many questions about the cabin that Mitch suggested they go explore it before continuing their float. Willow tried to beg off, but Mitch and the children pulled her after them to cross the river. Tyler was already climbing the bank, looking for the best path to reach the cabin. When he was sure that Willow was following, Mitch took the lead, skirting the edge of the field under the bluff where the walking was easier. Barney raced delightedly between Mitch and the children. When it looked like he was completely passing the cabin above them and heading toward the farm buildings, Mitch turned left onto a narrow trail up through the trees. Without knowing it was there, anyone passing by would have missed it.

Mitch led them up the steep winding path that led to the crest of the ridge. With one child in front and the other behind Tyler, they pulled and pushed him up the trail. Willow brought up the rear. Instead of the soft, rich dirt of the bottom field, the ground became gravelly, then almost solid rock when they climbed the final switchback to see the cabin. Before them stretched the open trail Tyler had seen from the river. No trees or bushes could grow on the broad shelves of layered rock outcroppings that, like slightly raised steps, hugged the fairly flat space at the crest of the ridge.

"Incredible," Tyler said. "I wish I'd brought my sketch pad."

"Just some ol' rocks," Cory said, running ahead to the cabin. About halfway there he stumbled, rolled over, and jumped to his feet. His tumble gave Dawn the advantage she needed to edge ahead of him. As if to justify to Tyler why Dawn outran him, he kicked at the stone and said, "This ol' rock moved and

And Tyler, Too?

tripped me." When Tyler grinned at him, the boy raced after his cousin.

Willow was enjoying watching Tyler's reactions. His childlike wonder was so infectious that she studied the familiar scene more carefully. It was like a storybook picture of rusticity. The weathered oak log building sagged in one corner as if too weary to stand erect any longer. The incongruous tin roof her father put over the wooden shingles several years ago was streaked with rust, which blended in with the grayish-brown of the aged logs. The windows were boarded up to cover the long-gone glass. By the corner of the house was a metal hand pump over a well curb of one big stone. Tall oaks, hickories, and walnuts crowded around the cabin on three sides. Only the front facing the natural rock road was open, giving those standing in the doorway a panoramic view across the river and far beyond to the forested mounds of blue hills.

When they reached the rock trail, the children and collie raced ahead, impatient with Tyler's slow pace. He stopped at almost every step to look.

"Incredible," Tyler said again. When looking at the view or anything he might want to memorize to sketch later, he held his head up, looking boldly. When Willow joined him, he turned to her, tilting his head down and to the right just slightly. He glanced at her as if looking over nonexistent glasses. "I've got to come back here and do some sketching."

"Sure, any time." He continued to look at her. She admitted to herself that he really did have charm. Every time he glanced at her from under his eyebrows like that she experienced a strange sensation.

"C'mon," Dawn and Cory were calling. "Come

see the cabin." They were standing in the door Mitch had pushed open.

Entering the cabin was like stepping back more than a century. Even the cobwebs that covered the few pieces of rough, homemade furniture were ancient. Tyler gave a single gasp and systematically ran his eyes over the one big room. His hand squeezed Willow's.

She enjoyed watching Tyler's reaction. He automatically reached to his pockets for his pencil and pad, laughing when he realized he was wearing only shorts, still wet from the river. Being here with Tyler was different from her last visit with Mitch—how long ago? Maybe fifteen years. In front of them was where they had their private playhouse when they were children. Some of their broken pottery dishes were still on the grime-covered table.

Though Tyler and Willow didn't move, Cory chased Dawn up the ladder to the loft that made a ceiling for half of the room.

"When was the last time anyone lived here?" Tyler asked.

"Grandma Edna never left it. She died at age ninety-two in 1923. No one has lived here since. Here's even some of her furniture that her husband made for her."

Tyler surveyed the walls and ceiling. "This should be preserved." Then he grinned, realizing that it *had* been preserved. "No, I mean someone should restore it." He grabbed Willow's arm and pulled her across the big room to examine the rock fireplace. "It wouldn't take much." He looked up the chimney, tapped on the log walls, and stomped on the puncheon floor. "It's all solid." Then he looked at Willow from under his lowered head. "Wouldn't it be fun?"

Willow had never thought about it. Yes, it would be fun. "Mom has some old photographs of Grandma Edna in front of the house taken in the 1920s. Her mother told us many times where she had everything." Willow was beginning to get excited. "We could restore it, couldn't we, Mitch, and refurnish it almost like it was?"

Mitch was also enjoying Tyler's enthusiasm. "Yes, we could." He moved from his spot at the door to look around. "I've got some old stuff that we could use to finish furnishing it."

"Mitch is an auctioneer," Willow told Tyler, as if that explained why he had old furnishings.

At Tyler's questioning look, Mitch said, "Lots of times at auctions when no one bids, or the bid is too low, I buy stuff that I think I can sell at the Saturday-night auction."

"Yeah," Willow said. "And he is a real softy on old stuff. He keeps it."

"I got a load of handmade cedar shingles a while back," Mitch said. "Just the thing to restore the roof back to the way it was."

"Really," Tyler asked. "You mean someone still makes shingles by hand?"

"Yeah. I know how, too, and if there aren't enough, I can make some more."

"Mitch is quite a craftsman," Willow said. No wonder he and Tyler hit it off so well. They were both artists. "And he could make the rest of the furniture to fill out what's here, couldn't you Mitch?"

"Yeah."

"Could you teach me to make shingles? Could I help restore the cabin?" Tyler's enthusiasm was like Cory's.

"Sure. Come over anytime and we'll start."

"Great." Tyler almost danced around the room looking at everything. "It's a wonder this stuff wasn't stolen or vandalized." He ran his hand over the surface of the big, solid maple table.

"It's way up here on the ridge off the main road. No one comes here but us," Mitch said.

"Why did they build in such an out-of-the-way place?"

"Years ago this used to be the main road," Willow said. "It continues down back of here to the ford. When they built the county road, they completely bypassed this and built the bridge down the river a couple of miles."

"We better get moving," Mitch said, "or it will be dark before we make camp at Fall-in-Bluff."

"C'mon, kids," Willow said to the children who were still messing around in the loft. She turned to Tyler. "We can hike back on the old trail to the ford. That way we won't have to swim back across to the canoes."

Chapter Four

That night Cory crawled into Willow's lap, since Dawn had already taken Tyler's. The embers from the campfire were almost out, only glowing briefly when the breeze caught them. Around the group on the gravel bar the tents had sprung up like blue and orange mushrooms against the chartreuse background of willows. The moonlight striking the colorful plastic made them appear almost phosphorescent. The lounging campers could look at the moon either up in the sky or reflected in the water that rippled over the rocks as it curved around their gravel bar. Or they could look behind them at the black, jagged limestone bluff and the jumble of boulders at its feet that looked as if some giant hand had pushed them off the cliff above.

The children were quiet for the first time today. Full of their grandmother's chicken and potato salad, they, as all the adults, were enjoying the inactivity in one another's presence. Willow was ready to call it a day. Her unaccustomed physical activity had left her more tired than she wanted to admit.

Safe in Willow's embrace, Cory didn't jump at the unexpected sound of the hoot owl from the willow grove behind them, nor did Dawn fear the bat that swooped from the crevices of the bluff out over the river catching mosquitoes. Barney lay quietly beside her and Tyler.

Everyone was content to just relax after their successful float on the river. As scheduled, the four canoes pulled up on the gravel bar at Fall-in-Bluff Eddy where Jerry and Maggie were awaiting them. Welcome smells of frying chicken drifted over the river from the temporary campsite. The fire was just right for the skillet of chicken and the old-fashioned Dutch oven full of Maggie's biscuits.

After the good meal and when the children had told their grandparents in detail the events of the day, especially their visit to the old cabin on the ridge, there was a pause—the pregnant pause that the children knew would end with being told to go to bed. Willow sighed and started to get up.

"Tell us about Grandma Edna," Cory said. Willow knew his tricks to forestall the inevitable as long as possible. She never refused a bedtime story request.

Willow laughed. "You've heard the story a hundred times." She settled back and hugged Cory tighter.

"Yeah, tell us again," Dawn said, rousing. Like her cousin, she was fighting sleep.

"Please," Cory begged, his head against her shoulder, his face puckered into a pout, which always got his way with her.

Dawn said to Tyler, "Aunt Willow tells good stories."

"I'll bet she does," he said. "Yes, Willow, tell us. I haven't heard it. Now that I've seen her cabin, I should know her story."

"Mom should tell it," Willow said. She turned to

her parents, who like all of the adults were paired off, her dad's arm over Maggie's shoulder as she leaned against him. Charley and Gene were each stretched out on blankets with their heads in their wives' laps. Mitch and Amy were sitting close together. Only she and Mitch were seated alone, that was, until the children crawled into their laps. In a circle around the dying embers of the fire, the people were two by two, separated from the other couples, but held together by the reflections of the fire that blazed up occasionally with each gust of wind. The circle of light from the moon that found its way through the trees to the gravel bar highlighted them. It gleamed off the silver clasp in Dawn's hair and danced from the metal buckles of Jerry's overalls when he laughed.

Everyone looked at Willow in anticipation, even her family who all remembered the legend as well as she. Knowing she could never win against her family's combined strength, she laughed, and shifting Cory from her leg which was becoming numb with his weight, set him on the blanket in the circle of her bare legs.

"I heard this story from your grandmother," she said to the children, but looked at Maggie, "who heard it from *her* grandmother and on back many years."

"And now Aunt Willow is telling it to us," Dawn told Tyler, "and someday I'll tell it to my kids."

"Yes, Dawn. We're passing it on to you. You kids remember me telling you that it was a really bad time back then when people in this country were fighting one another over whether it was right to own slaves."

"This is a true story," Dawn told Tyler, "not a make-believe."

"That's right," Willow continued. "It really happened, but we're not sure what details may have been added in the telling over the years."

"But her house is still there. We saw it, didn't we?" Dawn asked.

"Yes," Willow said, "her house is still standing. No one wants to spend the money to repair it, but no one wants to tear it down, either."

"Go on, Aunt Willow," Cory said, pulling her arm. "Tell about the bad men."

"Grandma Edna and Grandpa Ben hadn't been married very long before the war started."

"That was the Civil War," Maggie said to Tyler, who nodded.

"Mother, of course he knows that."

"I thought he might not, being—"

"Let her tell it," Jerry said, patting his wife's hand.

"Yes, this happened during the Civil War. Grandma Edna and Grandpa Ben were pioneers and hadn't been in this area long. They bought a hundred and sixty acres there on the river, bottomland and ridge land. They were poor farmers with just one team of horses, some cows and pigs, a wagon, plow, and some tools. Together they built their house, made their furniture, and put out their crops. They didn't have slaves or have any interest in the politics about the war. They ignored the bits of news they heard about the war, because it was far away from their Ozark home. It didn't concern them, they thought. They were too busy making a home."

"Get to the bad men," Cory said, pulling on her arm. He yawned and leaned back against Willow. She put her arms around him as he nestled against her.

"Okay, I will. Be patient. Then one day in late July of 1861, a company of Union soldiers came by. Grandpa Ben was out in the woods cutting some logs to build another room onto their house because they were expecting a baby. Grandma Edna welcomed the soldiers, as everybody did back then when any stranger came by, and though there were ten or twelve of them, she fixed them a meal."

"She didn't know yet that they wanted Grandpa Ben," Dawn continued her explanation to Tyler.

"No, but she soon found out. They knew there was a man about somewhere, because a woman wouldn't be alone out there like that, and they saw men's clothing and stuff around the room. So they waited. After eating, they smoked and rested under the trees. When Grandpa Ben came to the house, the men surrounded him. They made him pack some clothes, get his shotgun, saddle his horse, and go with them.

"Of course, he didn't want to. But there were too many of them. Rather than fight there in the house and maybe hurt Grandma Edna, he went with them, planning to get away later and come back. 'It's just until we push the Rebels out of Missouri,' the lieutenant told Grandma Edna. 'Maybe a couple of weeks. Then he'll be back.'"

"But he didn't come back, did he?" Cory asked.

"Not for a while. Grandma Edna was left all by herself with only one half a team. She ran to her neighbors, but the same thing happened there. All the men were gone. Two weeks went by, and then two months. She heard stories of the big battle of Wilson Creek about seventy miles southwest of her. Hundreds of Union soldiers were killed, she heard, and the Union

Army had to retreat after their general was killed. A couple of times Union soldiers stopped by or she saw them at the general store, but she didn't hear anything about Grandpa Ben for a long time.

"In the fall she managed to pick most of the corn by rigging up a cart the one horse could pull, but a unit of Confederate soldiers came through and took her last horse and most of her corn. When she knew her baby was coming, she managed to walk to a neighbor. Her little girl was born there. A few days later when she came home, she saw that some bushwhackers—"

"That's the bad men," Dawn explained, stifling a yawn.

"That's right, Dawn. With all the men away at war, outlaws could do whatever they wanted. They stole everything they could use or sell. All her food, her blankets and comforters, all of Grandpa Ben's clothes, and even the chickens.

"Here she was alone with a brand-new baby and very little to keep house with. Neighbors always shared and helped, and though most of them had lost much, they shared some bedding and food. It wasn't too late for garden stuff. Grandma Edna dug sweet potatoes and turnips the bushwhackers didn't find. And she gathered some late beans they hadn't destroyed when they tromped through the garden looking for anything they could eat. She scoured the woods for nuts and roots she knew about. She fished in the river, the baby wrapped up in her one blanket lying on the bank beside her. Somehow the soldiers and outlaws had missed a shotgun lying on a jutting log on the wall. So she hunted rabbits and possums. To save the ammunition, she set rabbit gums."

And Tyler, Too?

"That's traps to catch 'em in," Cory said. "Daddy and I set some gums."

"Grandma Edna was able to catch enough to have meat for her. She didn't need much herself, but since she expected her husband to come back, she dried the extra meat and hid it. By this time she learned to keep hidden everything of value that she still had. Then, so the story goes, she began to get some letters from Grandpa Ben, but the details on this are rather vague. We assume she wrote back. Maybe he sent her some money, we don't know, but she survived the winter, and she knew he was still alive.

"Then one day in early February the next year, that was 1862, another detail of Union soldiers stopped by."

"These weren't the bad men," Dawn said sleepily.

"No. This time it was a happy meeting. Grandpa Ben was with this bunch. You can imagine how happy Edna was. His unit had been moving constantly since the hasty retreat of the Federals at Wilson Creek the August before. He had been to several places in south Missouri and had fought in several scrimmages. He was now stationed at Jefferson Barracks in St. Louis. He was a sergeant in charge of a small detail on his way to Springfield with a payroll in gold coins for the soldiers in southwest Missouri. They were once again on the offensive, preparing to push the Confederate Army out of Missouri."

Willow looked down at Cory, who was asleep in her arms. Dawn was also asleep. Their mothers carried the children to their tents.

"Not the usual bedtime story," she said to Tyler.

"Better than most. This is about their own family history," he said.

"They are fascinated with the story. But tonight they wanted you to hear it since we saw the old cabin."

"What happened next?" Tyler asked. "I gather the couple didn't live happily ever after."

"No."

"Tell me."

"Actually I haven't got to the best part," Willow said. With the children in bed, the adults moved closer as she continued.

"Of course, that time it was a happy meeting. Ben and his men did some chores around the house, brought in more wood, patched the roof, stuff like that. And according to the story, he gave Edna his saved wages. Ben and Edna made a quick trip to the store four miles away for supplies. At the store they heard that a Confederate unit was coming their way, apparently warned that the Union soldiers were somewhere in the area.

"They hurried back to the cabin and Ben alerted his men. Since he knew he couldn't reach Springfield through the Confederate patrols, he decided to return to the safety of St. Louis, which was firmly held by the Union. But as a precaution in case the Confederates should overtake them, Ben hid the bags containing the payroll. Thinking he would soon return and to protect his wife, he didn't tell her where he hid the money. The men stashed it in a big hurry, for they also needed to erase any evidence of their being on the farm and lay a false trail that bypassed the cabin.

"The false trail saved Edna and the cabin, but the

Confederates caught up with Ben. In an ambush, he and all of his men were killed."

"And no one knew where he hid the gold," Maggie finished for Willow.

"Is this for real?" Tyler asked, expecting to see them laughing at his gullibility.

"It's for real," Maggie said seriously. Everyone around the now-dead campfire nodded. The moon, now high in the southern sky, shined down on the group, highlighting the tight circle. Behind, the dark woods framed them. Before them the glints of moonlight on the ripples of the dark river danced with the current. An owl hooted in the distance. Tree frogs chirped, accompanied by the deep bass of two bullfrogs.

"A few years back," Maggie said, "I did some research through old army records. I'd heard the legend all my life, but hadn't paid much attention to it, like you, thinking it was just a good story. The hills are full of lost-treasure stories. I wanted to see if there was anything to it. Well, I found the records that stated that on February 1, 1862, Sergeant Benjamin Dawson—"

"That was Grandpa Ben," Mitch said.

"Yes. The records said that he was ordered to take a large payroll in gold coins to General John C. Frémont in Springfield. The report said the unit was pursued and overtaken. In the fight, all the men were killed and the payroll was confiscated."

"The official record is that the Confederates took the gold," Willow said.

"But how do you know your ancestor, this Dawson ... how do you know he hid it?" Tyler asked.

"The family legend says that he did. And that he told Edna he hid it," Willow said.

"Only not *where* he hid it, right?"

"Right. This is the part of the story that may be exaggerated or added on," Willow said. "You know, the romance of buried treasure. Maybe somewhere down the line, somebody tacked on the part about him hiding it before he left."

"We don't have any other evidence," Maggie said.

Tyler had stood up in his excitement. This story seemed real to him. He'd seen the actual Dawson cabin overlooking the river bottom. Here were these descendants of Ben and Edna to prove they really existed. His adventuring, seagoing blood called to him.

"And no one has ever found it?"

"No. It probably doesn't exist except in our stories," Mitch said.

"So if it's still somewhere around here, let's go look for it."

Everyone laughed at Tyler's enthusiasm. He looked as though he was ready at that moment to start searching.

"Sit down, Hugh," Jerry said. "Generations of people in Maggie's family have combed the area. Maggie and I did. So have Charley, Gene, Mitch, and Willow. I expect that little Cory and Dawn will come up with some new ideas of where to look when they get old enough."

"It's sort of a growing-up ritual in our family," Mitch said. "When we finally give up on finding ol' Ben's gold, we become adults."

"For some it took longer than others," Jerry said. "Maggie didn't give up until just before Willow was

And Tyler, Too?

born." He looked affectionately at his wife. She slapped playfully at his leg, shaking her head at what she knew he would say next.

Willow also groaned. "Now he'll tell how I got my name," she said.

Ignoring Maggie and Willow, Jerry said, "Maggie got the idea that the gold was in the crevices in this bluff right here. Did you notice how rough and pitted it is?" They all looked behind them, but could see very little in the darkness. When Tyler nodded, he continued. "Well, she got the notion that Ben hid it in this bluff before these rocks fell in. She thought it might be covered up from the bluff falling in."

Though from the growth around the bluff and the weathering of the stone, it was obvious that the rocks had fallen many years before Ben's time, Tyler said nothing.

Jerry continued, "She made me climb all over that bluff—she was pregnant, you know, so she couldn't do much climbing. She sat on a fallen log in that willow grove back there while I searched every hole I could get to and climbed all over these boulders."

"I was born later that night," Willow said.

"And though we had picked out a good family name, she named her Willow," Jerry said.

Tyler looked at Willow. "The name suits you."

"No, it doesn't. A willow bends and gives with the wind. I'm rigid and stubborn." Willow held her mouth tight to prove her point.

"A willow is graceful and light," Tyler said. "It can survive in almost any location, even in New York City, but it really flourishes here by the river. Even in the city it is beautiful, but here with the water running over its feet and the gray limestone cliffs behind it, it is the most beautiful of all."

Mitch whistled. Charley and Gene clapped. Jerry and Maggie exchanged satisfied glances.

"You guys," Willow said, embarrassed. She stood up. "I'm going to bed." She crawled into her tent and zipped up the opening.

"At the end of the first quarter the score is, Tyler one, Willow nothing," Mitch said loudly enough for Willow to hear.

Chapter Five

"It's my turn," Cory said. He and Dawn had been playing pioneer days. "Now I want to be Grandpa Ben when he comes back with the soldiers. I don't want to be the bad soldiers anymore."

"Okay," Dawn agreed. "I'll be in the cabin reading your letters and you come in. Wait a minute." She ran into her grandmother's house to the room she and Cory shared when they visited. She was soon outside again with a small package. She sat down cross-legged in the grass. "Okay."

Cory grabbed a stick and galloped up to her. In pantomime he held up his arm to halt his men, tethered his horse while giving orders, and strutted up to his cousin.

This was the morning of the day following their float trip. With much pleading and assurance from Willow that she really wanted them, the children's parents allowed them and Barney to stay with their grandparents for a few days. Willow was swinging in the porch swing, idly enjoying the children's playacting, and very much aware of Tyler's eyes constantly watching her. He was perched on the porch railing, absorbing the small-town activity around him without missing Willow's every movement and expression.

"I've come home from the war," Cory said, standing stiffly with a stick gun resting on his shoulder.

"And I was just reading your letters again," Dawn said. She was holding a package close to her body.

"You can't read," Cory said, out of character. Then his curiosity was aroused. "Let me see them." He grabbed at the package.

"No. I found them. They are mine."

"Where'd you find them?" He looked more closely. "Oh, that's the junk you found yesterday in Grandma Edna's cabin."

Dawn held out a small, yellowed parcel of papers tied with a faded rag strip. As Cory took them from her, the rotten rag string broke and the papers dropped to the ground.

"Wow!" Cory said. Both children got on their hands and knees to look. As the papers separated slightly from the fall, they could see tiny handwriting.

"What does it say?" Dawn asked Cory, who had been one year to kindergarten. Both children were on their hands and knees studying the papers.

Cory screwed up his face. "Here's an E, and I think that's a T. I can't read writing yet, just printing."

Willow was trying to sort out her feelings about Tyler's continued presence. After the float trip, her parents invited him to stay as long as he liked. She could never get away from him. But the surprising thing was that she didn't mind it. Her vacation was turning out to be better than usual. She was thriving on all the attention she was getting. In New York she was too busy carving out her career to have any social

And Tyler, Too?

life. Back in her hometown with three weeks of vacation ahead of her, she had all the time she wanted.

When Tyler was preoccupied watching the children at play or surveying the neighborhood on the edge of the town where her parents lived, she looked closely at him. She had to pick her times, for usually she caught his eyes on her when she glanced his way.

Here away from the arty scene of New York, Tyler seemed a different person. He still had his long hair, but instead of the bold, layered clothes of the city, he wore tan slacks and a plain-colored T-shirt. Already resigned to the fact that everyone in her family liked him, she relaxed her guard. He wasn't the stuck-up city snob she had pegged him. From snatches of conversation she remembered from her parents' visit in her office and subsequent times, she realized that he hadn't always lived in New York. Was it Italy? Or maybe Portugal? She was guilty of stereotyping him because of his New York art connections. She remembered when she first moved to the city how she resented being labeled a hick because of her Ozark background. She'd have to find out more about him.

"I am back, my wife," Cory said, standing up and resuming his playacting. "My men will protect you." He gave an order to Barney, as one of his men. "But wait." He paused dramatically and listened. "I think I hear the Rebels coming. I'll hide this gold and then I'll save you."

Cory galloped off on his stick horse waving his "gun." "Follow me, men," he said. Barney ran at his heels while Dawn gathered up the bundle of papers.

"Aunt Willow," she said, looking up and seeing Willow and Tyler watching from the porch, "why can't I ride after the soldiers like Cory? All I do is fix his supper.''

Willow laughed. ''Well, remember this. Cory is going to get killed and you live a long life. If you rode off with him, then you'd get killed and we wouldn't know anything about you.'' She glanced at Tyler to see his reaction.

''Good point.'' He laid his hand over hers. His strong fingers intertwined with hers.

Dawn's forehead wrinkled in thought. ''Yeah. And then no one would ever see these letters.'' She carefully picked up the papers.

''No,'' Willow humored her, trying to keep her mind on the child while unusual sensations were coursing through her from Tyler's touch. ''Are those the letters that Grandpa Ben wrote?'' She was glad of Dawn's presence, which meant she didn't have to address the feel of his hand.

''Yes, these are my love letters,'' Dawn said, her dimple deepening.

Tyler tightened his hold on Willow's hand slightly. They exchanged glances of amusement as they both entered into the children's play.

Finding that going off by himself to fight the enemy wasn't as much fun as the attention Dawn was getting, Cory returned, riding his stick horse and imitating the sounds of horse hooves. Seeing a scrap of yellowed paper that Dawn hadn't picked up, he swooped down to retrieve it. He reined his horse to study the paper. Unable to read what it said, he galloped up to the porch bannister and handed it to Willow. Still in her playacting mood, she read off, '' 'My most precious possession.' ''

And Tyler, Too?

She and Tyler exchanged serious glances. No way could the children have written those words. And a cursory glimpse at the papers Dawn was holding showed them that they were not written by the same hand. Together they ran down the steps to look more closely at the papers Dawn clutched in her hand.

"May I see one of those papers?" Tyler asked Dawn. She readily gave him one. He glanced at it hurriedly, turned it over, and then handed it to Willow. She took a good look, her eyes opened wide in amazement. Brushing a strand of hair from her eyebrow, she glanced at Tyler. "What do you think, Tyler? Could it be hers?"

"Could be," he almost whispered. He was studying the other papers.

"Where'd you get these?" Willow asked in her executive New York voice as she grabbed Dawn. Her tone was sharp and excited, almost accusing, quite a contrast to her usual indulging-aunt voice.

Thinking she'd done something wrong, Dawn whimpered, "Nowhere." She hung her head. Tears sprung into her eyes.

"She found them in the cabin yesterday," Cory said. If anyone was going to get into trouble, he wanted them to know he had nothing to do with it.

"Where, Dawn?" Willow asked, controlling her excitement. "It's all right. I didn't mean to scold you. You may have found something very important."

She gathered the child into her arms to comfort her. When Tyler lifted his eyes from the papers, he caught Willow's questioning look. He nodded.

"Where'd you find them, pumpkin?" Willow asked

again. This time she lost her demanding voice and was again the loving aunt.

"Under that board in the loft," Cory answered for her.

" 'Member, I told you there was a loose board?" Dawn asked Willow.

Willow nodded.

"And you told us to get down before we tripped and fell?" Cory said.

When Willow nodded, Dawn continued, "Well, we didn't right away. You were looking at stuff downstairs, so we pulled out the board."

"Dawn did," Cory said, "and under it was this little hole."

"With these papers," Dawn finished for him.

When Willow didn't answer but stared at her, Dawn again puckered up her mouth, hung her head ready to cry, and pouted. "Grammy always said we could have anything we found in the cabin. She lets us play with the old-time stuff."

"Yes, pumpkin, that's all right. What's in the cabin is as much yours as anyone's."

"Was there anything else in the hole?" Tyler asked.

Both children had blank looks. "Don't know."

"How big was it?"

Cory held out his hands about ten inches apart.

"Too small for the gold," Willow said to Tyler. He nodded. "Besides, we've gone over the place with a Geiger counter."

"Then you just carried these papers out and no one saw you?" Willow asked Dawn.

"I saw her," Cory said.

"I didn't hide them." Dawn was almost crying again. "I just took them out."

"How'd you get them across the river without getting them wet?"

Tyler answered that one. "I carried her on my shoulders, don't you remember? Mitch was in a hurry to get going."

"Are those really Grandma Edna's letters?" Cory asked. "Like it says in the story that she got some letters from him to let her know he wasn't killed?"

"I believe they are," Tyler said. He answered the boy, but talked to Willow. "This paper is quite old and the kind that was used in the mid-1800s. Good-quality paper. Today's paper would have deteriorated by now. But protected between the boards in the floor from the light and dampness, these letters have been preserved."

Willow ran her hand over the paper to feel its texture.

"And the ink," Tyler continued. "Look at the color of it, how it's faded. It is written in the old script style. See how when there is a double S in a word the first S is written sort of like an F? That's a very old style of writing. And the clincher. Here, look at this date—September 15, *1861*. This one begins, 'My dear wife.'"

Willow was leafing through to see if the writer used any names in the headings or closings. Each began with the same salutation and closed with "Your loving husband."

As Tyler talked, Willow's excitement mounted. "Mom, Dad," she called into the house. "Mom, come out here!" No one in Mansfield & Logan, Inc., of New

York City would recognize in their efficient and cool-headed fashion merchandiser this excited young woman yelling for her mother.

Wiping her hands on her apron, Maggie ran out the door, followed by Jerry. Both had worried expressions as if expecting that some terrible disaster had elicited such a summons.

"Mom, look what Dawn found yesterday in the old Dawson cabin." She held out the bundle of letters.

Puzzled, Maggie looked at her excited daughter, at Dawn, and then at Tyler for some explanation.

"They appear to be letters written from Ben Dawson to his wife," Tyler said. The corporate executive was tongue-tied with emotion, while the artist spoke with businesslike efficiency.

"Oh my!" Maggie said, twisting her apron. "Oh my!"

"Let's see them," Jerry said.

"The paper is very fragile and the letters seem to be in some order," Tyler said. "Perhaps we should go inside and spread them out on a table. If we handle them much more they will crumble."

"Me, too," Dawn said. "I found them. Can I come, too?"

"Yes, you too," Jerry said. "And Cory. Let's all go in and see what Dawn found."

When they had the papers spread out in the order they were tied, there were three letters beginning "My dear wife," and another single sheet in a different handwriting with no salutation.

"This one must be in Edna's handwriting," Maggie said, picking one up.

And Tyler, Too?

"Wait, Mom," Willow said, putting her hand over her mother's. "Let's read them in order."

Everyone agreed that Tyler should read them out loud. His familiarity with the script handwriting made him the logical choice, not to mention that he was the only one calm enough to read. Without touching the papers again except to turn them over to read the writing on the back, Tyler began with the first one.

September 15, 1861

My dear wife,

I am writing this though I do not know if you will ever receive it. Since I left I think only of you and how you are getting along. I'm sick worrying about you getting in the corn and tending to the cattle all by yourself. When your time comes, don't worry about the stock, but go to the Reeses'. They will help you with the baby. How I wish I was there with you.

I thought I could get away, or for sure come home after the Wilson Creek battle, but I see there's no use. The army would just take me again, and this time probably shoot me for desertion. Or the Rebels would find me. All the way to Springfield after we left you, the lieutenant took every man we came across just like he did me. It looks like now that I won't be home for a while. The war will last much longer than anyone thought.

Our unit didn't fight in the battle at Wilson Creek. We were stationed with Colonel Marcus Boyd to guard Springfield. But the fight was only a few miles away. We could hear the cannons.

The wounded and the retreating army came to us. We expected General Price to follow up his victory and capture Springfield, but he didn't. We soon left Springfield and we've been running across the southern part of the state ahead of the Rebels and sometimes slowing them down.

My love, I hold you in my heart always. Don't worry about me. You are the brave one, the one most in danger. I'm with my regiment and we know who our enemies are and usually we know where they are. But you are all by yourself facing dangers from all sides—even from our own army.

May our loving Father protect you until I return. As always I remain your loving husband.

When Tyler finished the first letter he looked up at Maggie. "Did your research tell you about Dawson's movements?"

"No. The first mention I found of him was in St. Louis just before he carried the payroll."

"We assumed he was in the battle at Wilson Creek, but apparently he was not," Willow said.

"It's not surprising," Jerry said. "Union General Lyon didn't trust anyone from Missouri. He thought they were all Rebels at heart, so he didn't send the local units in. It's logical that Ben would have been assigned to guard Springfield."

"It was a terrible time," Maggie said.

The children were bored with all this adult talk. Cory tried to get Dawn to join him and continue their play outside, but since she had found the letters, she wanted to stay. She climbed onto Tyler's lap. "Does it say anything more about the baby?" she asked.

And Tyler, Too?

"Let's read on and see," he said, balancing her on one leg as he carefully unfolded the next letter.

October 14, 1861

My dear wife,

I can hardly get through each day what with worrying about you and wondering how you are. The baby should be here by now. Last night when I was on guard duty and everyone else was asleep, I thought how easy it would be to slip away. I could reach you in a few days. To see you and hold you and be with you is all I want in life. But I dared not. Last week a homesick private from Rolla ran off. The lieutenant himself chased him down. They brought him back to camp and hung him for all of us to see. I'll be no good to you and the baby dead, so I'll bide my time.

I'm saving my wages to give you when I see you. We'll just have to get through this and look forward to better times.

Don't worry about me. We're on the move all the time, mostly scouting out the Rebels. We've only been in a couple of scrimmages. Nothing serious. I hear that we're headed to St. Louis. Maybe I can volunteer as a clerk or something. Hardly any of the recruits can read or write, so I'll probably have a good chance.

Did you name the boy after me? Or was it a girl? I hope it is a girl. Then she will never have to fight in a war. How I wish I could see you both, to be with you. I know that there's plenty of wood there for the gathering, and with the corn and fall garden, I pray that you can survive the winter.

Blessings to you and the baby from your loving husband.

Tyler laid the letter beside the first one. No one said anything. Maggie wiped the tears from her eyes. Jerry cleared his throat. From outside, Cory's loud orders to his "horse" and his simulated "bang, bang" filled the silence when Tyler stopped reading.

"He didn't even know the baby was a girl," Dawn said, looking at each of the adults around her, wondering why they were so silent.

"No, Dawn," Willow said. "He hadn't heard anything since the soldiers took him away from home about three months earlier."

"Why didn't he just call her on his cellular phone?"

The laughter broke the pensive mood. Dawn puckered up her lips ready to cry. Willow knelt beside her and held her hand. "Pumpkin, that was a long time before there were any telephones or radios or even cars. The bad soldiers were all around, and there was no way for Grandpa Ben to get word to his wife."

The child frowned as she tried to envision such a world. Then she brightened up. "Oh, like in the Bible times?"

"Well, yes, sort of, only not that long ago."

"Let's hear the rest of the letters," Maggie said.

"They won't tell where he hid the gold, for this was before he ever brought it," Jerry said. "And if the stories are true, he certainly didn't write to her after he left that last time."

"And if he had, Edna would have found the gold long ago," Willow said.

"I know, I know." Maggie slapped Jerry affectionately on his arm and smiled at Willow. "This is a love story as well as a mystery."

"I'm for that," Tyler said. Before he picked up the third letter, he sneaked a look at Willow, catching her looking at him. He grinned.

Everyone at the table could see that there was only one more letter remaining, plus the short note in a different handwriting on a torn piece of paper resting by itself on the table.

Chapter Six

The group at the table was waiting expectantly as Tyler picked up the third letter. He studied the date. "I think it is dated January something. I can't make it out. It's 1862, though, that I can easily see." He showed it to Maggie, who agreed.

While everyone waited for him to begin the last letter, he took a moment to scan it first. Then he said, "Under the date is written, 'Jefferson Barracks, St. Louis.' And just like the others this one begins, 'My Dear Wife.' "

I haven't been able to write you because we've been on the move all the time. I wrote several letters but couldn't post them. I have a chance now to send this, so I'll write a few words. I am in St. Louis. It's much better here, for we are in a permanent fort. As I hoped, I am doing some clerical work. Presently I am with the paymaster. You needn't worry about me as I'm not in any danger. If I stay here longer, I'll try to move you and the baby here until the war is over. (I still haven't heard from you to know how he is, or she? And you? I worry all the time.) Some of the

And Tyler, Too?

men have families living in St. Louis. It'd be safer for all of us.

The paymaster sends the payroll to troops around the state. I'll volunteer to lead the detail the next time it goes to Springfield. Since our place is pretty much on the way, I will stop by and maybe bring you back with me then. Oh, if only that can happen.

Until then, I am your loving husband.

When he stopped reading, his eyes sought Willow's. She was motionless, her eyes glued to the floor.

"His love of Edna caused his death!" Maggie said. There were tears in her eyes. "If he had stayed in St. Louis, he wouldn't have been killed."

Willow was thinking exactly the same thing—how a scheme to see a loved one could backfire and affect the lives of many others. Even down to her, five generations later.

"If, if," Jerry said. "We can't be thinking about what if. It happened. But look at the whole picture. It was still early in the war. Ben likely would have been sent to the action that was building up in the south or to the east. Many Missouri men were at Shiloh, Chickamauga, and even with Sherman all the way to the sea. The likelihood of his surviving would have been poor. I read somewhere that of all the men from Missouri who went to war, only—"

"Yes, Dad, we know," Willow interrupted. An avid Civil War buff, Jerry loved to talk about it, sometimes boring his listeners with facts and figures. She didn't want to lose the feeling of Ben's letters. "We know that all kinds of things might have happened to him even if he wasn't killed on that payroll assignment." She still did not meet Tyler's eyes.

"Well, we already knew for sure that he got the assignment with the payroll," Maggie said. "Now we know more about him. Up to his carrying the payroll, these letters have documented the family story."

"That doesn't mean that the hidden gold part is true," Jerry said, his hand on his hip and his head tilted to the side. "That's the part that could easily be tacked on to the story by people telling it later."

"I know, I know," Maggie said. She turned to Tyler. "Jerry showed me a story in a recent book of lost treasure stories of the Ozarks that was almost identical to ours."

Jerry nodded as if that proved his point. "Yes, a payroll intended for soldiers was hidden quickly and then the men ambushed and nobody ever found it."

"It could have happened more than once. Or maybe the researcher of that book heard of our story," Maggie said. "Lots of people know about it. Maybe he heard it and the story in the book is *our* story. That doesn't mean that it's not true."

"She's right, Dad," Willow said. "Our story dates back over a hundred years before this book was written. It doesn't discredit our story. It may just mean that the author really did some digging and found our story. I believe it was written up in the county paper several years back, wasn't it, Mom?"

"Yes." Maggie's enthusiasm was becoming contagious.

"Perhaps," Tyler said with almost as much enthusiasm, "it has entered the lore of the region more than

And Tyler, Too? 63

you know. My dad told all kinds of folk stories about the sea and his—"

"Yes," Willow said, looking at her mother and Tyler in turn. She was catching their spirit. "Like Spanish silver hidden in the hills."

"Or sunken Portuguese galleons full of the wealth of the Far East," Tyler said. Willow sent him a guarded look, wondering why he mentioned an example from such a distant part of the world. Sunken Spanish ships loaded with Aztec gold from Mexico would have been more to the point—geographically, at least.

"Exactly," Jerry said. He understood why Tyler used this example. "There are tales of hidden wealth in all cultures and from ancient Greek times. They just become updated to suit the present political and geographical scene. Your family, Maggie, heard folk tales of hidden treasure, and somewhere along the line these stories got moved to the Ozarks and the Civil War scene. From there it was easy to tack it on to Ben Dawson."

Dawn left Tyler's lap, impatient with all this discussion. In the bundle she found in the old cabin there was one more paper still lying on the table unread. She picked it up, screwing her face to make some sense of it. She pulled at Willow's sleeve to get her attention. When that didn't work, she climbed back onto Tyler's lap, the paper in her hand. She put her face right up to his and said, "Uncle Tyler, read me the last letter."

Willow cringed at her use of "uncle."

Maggie laughed. "From the mouths of babes. But she's right to the point. All this talk doesn't get us anywhere. Maybe this last sheet will clear up some things."

"Okay, Dawn," Willow said. And making a big deal to indicate that she omitted the "uncle," she said, "*Tyler* will read it now."

Tyler, obviously flattered when Dawn called him uncle, and trying to ignore Willow's objection to it, took the letter from the child. He settled her in his lap and held the paper up for all to see. "As we all can tell, Ben didn't write this one. There's no date." He turned it over to the back, which was blank. "There's no salutation or signature and part of it seems to be torn off."

"Probably Grandma Edna's," Maggie said. "What does it say?"

Tyler began reading more slowly than before, as this handwriting was tiny and more difficult to decipher. He glanced at Willow and caught her eyes before she lowered them.

> *Just afore Ben and his soldiers left, he said some strange words to me. I didn't give it no mind at the time, but since then I've been studying on them, and I've about decided that they was not about us so much as about the payroll that he was carrying. He didn't say nothing to me about what he was doing that morning after we got back from the store afore he left in such a hurry, but I thought then and still do now that he did something with the payroll. The report was that the Rebels knew they had it and they took it after ambushing and killing everybody. I don't think they found the payroll. Best I remember after all*

these months, this is what he said—You and the baby are the rock foundation of my life. Wherever I travel on the road of life, I will treasure you. I hope to return, but if I don't, I want you to find comfort in the richness of our love.

I'm writing this down so I can...

"Don't stop now," Maggie said. She had stood up in her eagerness to hear every word.

"That's all there is," Tyler said. "The paper is torn here." Once again he turned the fragile paper over to see if there was more writing. Seeing none, he looked to Willow as if she knew what the missing words would be.

Willow took the paper to see for herself.

"See?" Maggie beamed at her husband. "There *was* a treasure. Grandpa Ben said so."

"Well, his use of the word 'treasure' does not necessarily mean money. It's all in metaphors," Jerry said.

"Read it again," Willow said, handing the paper back to Tyler. "Just the words Grandpa Ben said."

In a steady, unemotional voice, Tyler read, " 'You and the baby are the rock foundation of my life. Wherever I travel on the road of life, I will treasure you. I hope to return, but if I don't, I want you to find comfort in the richness of our love.' " Tyler emphasized the words "treasure" and "richness."

"See?" Maggie repeated to her husband when Tyler drew the same conclusions she did from the reading.

Jerry shrugged, unconvinced. "It wasn't a tape transcription. She said herself that it was months after he said them that she wrote them down, and I quote her, 'Best I remember after all these months, this is what he said.' She could have put the word 'treasure' in there herself.''

Maggie wrinkled up her nose at him.

Just as Edna Dawson did almost a hundred and forty years before, so did the group around the table "study" on the words Ben said. Except Dawn. She ran out the room, calling Cory.

"Cory, Grandpa Ben did hide a treasure. I found a letter that said he did!"

Cory quickly left his play to join her. Excitedly Dawn said, "He kissed Grandma Edna and the baby good-bye and told her to look for the treasure and be happy."

"Wow!" Cory said. "Where is it?" He was ready to go right after it.

Dawn's smile changed into a frown, and then into a pout. "He didn't say." Then she brightened. "But we know that the gold was hidden. We just need to find it."

A true grandson of Jerry Hill, Cory struck the same pose Jerry used to discredit Maggie's assurances. With his hand on his hip and his head cocked to one side, he said, "That don't help any. Everybody has already looked everywhere."

"Cory is right," Willow said. "Grandpa Ben didn't tell where it was."

Jerry was rereading Ben's words. "I grant that you might infer from this that he hid the payroll, but he doesn't actually say so. Taken at its face value it says that Edna and the baby were the center of his life, that while away from them he will use them as his anchor.

But he's realistic enough to know that he may be killed. And if he is, he wants them to continue their lives and keep alive the memories of their life together.''

"Yes," Willow said, "that is a logical interpretation. The literal one. That's what he wanted the soldiers around him to think he meant. With them there, he didn't have an opportunity to tell Edna without them knowing it. It was army money, you remember, not his.''

"Not only that," Tyler said, "but he probably didn't want her to figure out immediately that he meant to protect her. What she didn't know wouldn't hurt her."

"That's right," Maggie said, beaming at him.

"Am I the only one that sees this for its face value?" Jerry asked.

"I'm afraid so, Dad," Willow said. "Read it again. Those are stilted words for a pioneer farmer to say as he kissed his wife good-bye—maybe forever. More like some romantic poet. He must have some other meaning he was wanting to tell her."

"That's what Grandma Edna thought, too," Maggie said.

"He probably was figuring out what he would tell her while he was hiding the money," Willow said.

"Let's go look for the money." Cory pulled on Willow's arms, trying unsuccessfully to get her to stand up. Dawn pulled Tyler. Obligingly he arose.

"Quiet, children," Maggie said. "Not now."

"Why not?" Tyler said, his eyes full of the excitement of a possible adventure. He cocked his head and looked at Willow with his captivating expression. "You game?"

With Tyler on their side, the children clambered over Willow, begging her to come. This time the two of them succeeded in pulling her up out of her seat.

"Sure, why not?" she agreed, throwing out her arms. This was crazy, but so was everything else on this vacation home. Spur-of-the-moment jaunts were not her style. Details needed to be carefully planned. Chasing off after ancient treasure on a whim was foreign to her nature.

But so was having Tyler around her for the past four days. And the children dogging every step. It was almost as if she and Tyler were already parents with two kindergarten-age children.

She had no plans what to do with Tyler for the rest of the day, or for that matter however long he planned to stay. He evidenced no move to leave. Until Dawn had brought out the bundle of letters, her conversation with him had become strained. Everyone else seemed in league to keep them alone together, except for the children. Willow was grateful for their presence to ease over the awkwardness she felt. Nothing seemed to bother Tyler, she noticed. He was totally absorbed in whatever was going on around him, enjoying every minute.

Heck, why not try again? Heading up a new search might be interesting. With the input of new ideas from Tyler and the children, maybe they would turn up something. Hadn't her father said at their camp on the river that Cory and Dawn might come up with some new ideas of where to look for the money when they got old enough? Certainly Tyler would have some fresh ideas.

She admitted to herself that she was beginning to resent the attention Tyler was getting. Perhaps that was part of her bad mood. This was *her* family and *her* precious few days at home. They were giving him all of their attention.

"I'll fix you some lunch," Maggie said, disappearing into the kitchen. She called back through the open double doors, "You can take Jerry's pickup, Willow. You'll need the four-wheel-drive to get to the cabin."

When Jerry nodded, Willow said, "Okay, Mom."

"The first thing would be to look in the hole Dawn found to see if there are any more papers. Right?" Maggie popped out into the dining room and directed the last word to Tyler.

"Right," he said. "And this time I'm taking my backpack of art supplies."

"And you all better put on some sturdy walking shoes," Maggie said. "Better change from those shorts to jeans. Lots of briars and weeds."

Jerry held up his hands in defeat and laughed. "She'll be telling you to take some bug spray next."

Back in the kitchen where she was slapping together some ham-and-cheese sandwiches, she yelled, "And Willow, get that new can of insect spray from the shelf in the bathroom, and watch out for poison ivy."

"Yes, Mom."

"What'd I tell you?" Jerry laughed, with everyone joining him.

Maggie ran out again, only this time she hugged Willow tightly and whispered, "I'm so glad to have you home."

Her father hugged them both. "You bet, honey." Then he spoiled the beautiful scene, by poking her and pointing to Tyler. "Don't let that one get away."

"Dad!"

Chapter Seven

"Are you sure we can drive all the way?" Tyler asked. They had just left the fairly decent gravel road they had traveled from the highway to Maggie and Jerry's farm. He got out to open the gate behind the barn that led across the bottom. After going through another less sturdy gate, they followed a rarely used trail that climbed the ridge.

The children were happily chattering to each other, Barney was delighted to be with them, his head looking around the cab from his perch in the back of the pickup, and Willow was driving with no more concern than if she were on a level paved highway. The red Chevy truck bounced. As she swerved unexpectedly to avoid holes or a fallen log, the children were thrown against Tyler; he bumped into Willow. Without slowing the truck, Willow reached out with her right hand to steady him.

She was laughing. This was her element. The past two days on the river were great, but she was still hung up on her disappointment in not being able to visit with Mitch. And Tyler's presence? By now she had accepted his company, was even beginning to enjoy it. She purposely drove a bit faster than she normally would to show off her driving skill and knowledge of the backwoods.

Her hand still on Tyler's arm, she steered the pickup back into the tracks after a rocky detour to avoid a chug hole. It felt right to leave her hand there. She moved it when she needed to shift into a lower gear when the road started up a grade.

"Hold on, everyone," she said cheerfully. The trail led almost straight up the hill. Years of rainwater running off the hill had gouged out ruts that crisscrossed the road. In places the ruts followed the tracks in the road. Gravel washed out from the thin topsoil was piled haphazardly along the way. Occasionally she had to detour around an exposed flat rock too large to drive over.

"Can you drive all the way?" Tyler repeated. When Willow did not answer his question, he suggested, "Perhaps we should walk the rest of the way."

"No problem," Willow said. "We're almost there."

She was greatly enjoying his reaction. Years of success in New York had not completely erased her need to prove to city people her expertise, her worth—even if she did come from these hills. Not only was she confident on Thirty-fourth Street and Seventh Avenue, she was queen of the back roads and streams of the Ozarks. She was warming more to him with each new experience.

His amazement and interest in the country from the seat of the truck cab was as enthusiastic as from the front of the canoe. At the crest of the hill they left the woods for an open glade covered with grasses and low brush. Willow stopped the truck for them to appreciate the view.

Below they could see the river bottom fields—a newly cut field of hay and the rich black soil showing under the rows of young corn and soybean plants. Coming from the distance and disappearing under the bluff below them, the double lines of trees almost hid the river, except in a few breaks in the trees where the sun sparkled off the water.

"Look, Uncle Tyler," Cory said, pointing on up the trail, "there's Grandma Edna's house." Willow still cringed when the children insisted on saying *Uncle Tyler.*

They all looked up the ridge to the cabin. "Is this where we climbed from the river the other day?" Tyler asked.

"Yeah," Cory said. "We came up that path." He pointed to their left and over the crest of the ridge.

"We're on top of the bluff," Willow said as she put the Chevy in gear to let it creep forward slowly.

"Why don't we walk?" Tyler said. He was uncomfortable. Just to the left of the truck was the edge of the bluff. Willow was driving now on the solid rock they had walked over, where even surefooted Cory had fallen. The layers of rock ascended to the cabin in irregular spacings like giant steps. Loose gravel that caused the tires to spin was scattered throughout. Stunted cedar trees and other low vegetation forced Willow to switch directions as she bumped forward. Once, the pickup tilted to the side, but quickly righted itself on a more solid track.

"Okay, Tyler, you can relax," Willow said, stopping and turning off the engine. "We're here, anyway."

The children and Barney jumped out and raced ahead to the cabin, just as they had done before on the float trip. "If you find anything else in the hole, Dawn," Willow called, "don't touch it. Wait for us."

"Okay."

Willow and Tyler ran to catch up with the children. They all climbed the ladder to the small loft and crowded around Dawn as she looked into the hole in the floor.

"I don't see anything more," she said.

Willow knelt down and put her hand in to feel around. Nothing. She lay prone so she could grope the length of her arm. Still nothing. When she moved back, Tyler stuck in a flashlight and shined its beam up and down the empty space between the joists. Only dust.

"I really didn't expect to find anything else," Willow said, though she was disappointed. "Except maybe the rest of Grandma Edna's note. I thought maybe Dawn tore it off when she pulled out the package."

"Wouldn't it be great if we found a diary or some more letters?" Tyler asked.

"I'll say. I thought this cabin had been thoroughly searched, but obviously not."

" 'Cause I found Grandpa Ben's letters, didn't I, Aunt Willow?"

"You certainly did, pumpkin. And just maybe there is more here." She turned to Tyler. "You see, we never thought to look for any letters. Always before we were looking for the payroll, which was gold coins.

Even the documentation Mom found said 'gold coins.' When we were in high school Mitch even rented a Geiger counter. We went all over the house, floors, walls, ceiling, and outside. We spent several days with it. All we found in the house were some old homemade nails, belt buckles, and some of those metal fasteners and buttons from overalls."

"Did you find anything interesting outside?"

"Naw. Just pieces of machinery, iron pans, and other discards from farming and housekeeping. Not even any antiques worth anything."

Willow studied the construction of the loft floor. Rough four-by-fours formed the foundation for the eight-by-ten-foot open space under the highest point of the roof. Wide, hand-hewn boards formed the floor of the loft. Underneath, duplicate boards fastened to the underside of the joists formed the ceiling of the portion of the downstairs that it covered.

Sending Cory to the truck for some tools, she and Hugh pried up boards enough to see if there was anything secreted away under them. After an hour of searching, they agreed there was nothing more hidden in the loft floor.

Outside in the shade of the lone oak tree that managed to find a foothold in the glade, they ate Maggie's lunch on the biggest of the many flat rocks. They were all glad to get out of the cabin to let the dust settle.

"Okay, kids," Willow said while they were finishing the cookies and apples, "this is your first time to look for the payroll. Now, in addition to the money itself, we're looking for any more papers that might help us find the money. Where would you look?"

The children looked at each other and grinned in

pleasure that an adult would ask their opinion. Since they had heard the stories of many other searches, they knew they should come up with new possibilities.

But they were stumped. The first time they were consulted, and they couldn't think of anything. Both children remained silent, their foreheads wrinkled in thought.

"Maybe," Cory said after careful consideration, "there could be some papers in the floor of the cabin like there was in the loft floor."

"Good idea," Willow said to encourage him. She knew that wasn't a possibility, but she wanted him to discover that himself. "Go take a look and see what you think."

Cory and Dawn ran into the cabin and stomped on the floor in several places to see if there were any loose boards. Not finding any, Cory ran outside and peered under the house through a gap in the rock foundation. With a hangdog expression, he returned to Willow and Tyler, who were still sitting on the rock beside the empty lunch basket.

"There's no other boards under the floor like up in the loft," he said. "No place to hide anything."

"That was a good thought, though, Cory," Tyler said. "We can cross that off the list." Cory smiled.

"What about the roof?" Cory suggested, then shook his head to answer his own question. The rafters of the roof were open to the inside with no interior plaster, lathing, or ceiling boards.

"Well, what about in the walls of the house?" Dawn said. Most of the interior walls were the backside of the chinked logs that formed the cabin, but in

And Tyler, Too?

a couple of places there was some walling covering the logs.

"Yeah," Cory said.

This time Willow and Hugh followed the children inside. Willow explained to Hugh, "Mom said her mother told her that even though Grandma Edna lived until 1923, she wouldn't let anyone make any improvements in the cabin. She kept it just as Ben had built it. However, in her later years, she did allow some wall covering on the north side of the cabin behind her bed to help keep out the wind."

Hugh examined the old-fashioned tongue-and-groove ceiling boards tacked on the wall. "Not a very tight job. I think we can probe behind here without tearing it all off," he said.

Using knotholes and boards that were already rotted or loose, they carefully pulled back strategic boards enough to see behind them. It was dirty, painstaking work to probe into cavities filled with decades of dust and soot. The children soon tired of watching and ran off to play.

Thinking that they might sometime restore the cabin, Willow didn't want to destroy what remained. When they searched one area, they carefully replaced the boards. Though marks of their work were visible, they could later hide them with sanding and paint.

The excitement they felt that morning after reading Ben's letters was wearing off with the heavy, dirty work. When they had finished half of the wall, they no longer experienced the thrill that each new spot might hide some clue. They began talking, or Willow did. She told Tyler about her childhood on this farm when she had lived in the big house they had passed on their way. Since her brothers were several years older than she, her recital was full of Mitch, who was her main companion.

"You miss him, don't you?" Hugh said.

"Oh." Willow hadn't thought about that. "I guess so. But we grew up and he married. We went different ways."

"Sorry you went to New York?"

"No! Definitely not. What would I do here?"

"Mitch and your brothers seem to have done all right."

"Yes, they have." She thought about them. "And they are content and happy, I know. But Charley can run an automotive business here as well as anywhere, and there's plenty work here for Gene as an accountant. But it isn't for me. Not much future here in fashion merchandising. Unless squirrels wore clothes." She laughed and pointed to a pair of fox squirrels chasing each other through the trees.

"No, I guess not. Or unless you built a garment factory."

Willow laughed again. "Yeah, using what as capital? Rocks? That's what this country has the most of."

Tyler worked a while in silence. "I could do my work here. Probably as well as in New York."

"You'd soon be out of touch with trends and fashions here."

"Not really, in this age of telecommunications. And it's only two hours away by air. Many people who work in the city from Jersey or Connecticut take longer than that to get to work."

Willow didn't answer. Presently Tyler said, "I like it here."

And Tyler, Too?

"Well, you're on vacation. If you were here all the time, you'd soon get bored. You'd miss the excitement of New York."

"I've had more excitement in the few days I've been here than in years in the city."

Willow looked at him in wonder. "Excitement here? Peaceful, comforting, safe, yes, but exciting?"

"Sure. The float trip, this cabin, that murderous rocky road, the past calling so urgently, a real mystery to solve, and . . ." He stopped and looked straight into Willow's eyes. She did not lower her head as she had been doing when their eyes met. ". . . and you. In New York you are interesting and attractive. Efficient, smart, and alluring." In spite of herself, Willow blushed. "But here . . ." He waved his arm to encompass the cabin, the ridge, the river, and the entire Ozarks. ". . . here you are exciting, bubbling over with life, a knowing and loving aunt and a naive little girl all rolled into one amazing package."

Willow's embarrassment forced her to lower her eyes. No one had ever said anything like this to her.

"I'm embarrassing you," Tyler said.

"You *are* piling it on pretty thick."

"I'm sorry. But you asked. You can't help but know that I've always liked you. Your parents saw that right away and they put me up to coming."

"I know."

"Well, I'm just being an obliging guy and doing what they want me to do to pay for their hospitality. I understand that I'm the latest cog in their plot for finding a husband for you."

In spite of herself, Willow laughed. It was so ridiculous and old-fashioned.

"Oh, come on," she mumbled, embarrassed to be talking about it. "Let's just forget my family and their archaic ideas. We can be friends and enjoy this vacation together, can't we? Without . . ."

"Sure thing."

". . . without constantly reminding me of my family's silly notions?"

"You betcha."

"Good. Around here, Tyler, when an agreement is reached, people shake on it." She held out her hand. When he took it and squeezed it instead of shaking it, an unbidden spark coursed though Willow.

They worked in silence for a few seconds while Willow tried to resume her usual demeanor. Suddenly she looked up in alarm. "I haven't heard the kids for some time." She dropped the crowbar and ran out the door. "Dawn! Cory!"

When there was no answer, she ran around the cabin to the pickup, and then to the edge of the bluff. There was no sign of them or Barney. Beside her Tyler grabbed her hand.

"They probably just went exploring. Maybe they're looking for some other hiding places for the money."

"Yes, I the same as asked them to." She called their names again. "I was stupid, stupid. I should have watched them more closely. They might get hurt."

"The collie is with them," Tyler said. "They'll be all right."

"Here, Barney, here boy!" Willow called.

Silence.

"Where would they go?" Tyler asked.

"Either back down the road to the farmhouse or down to the river. You go down the bluff path to the

And Tyler, Too?

river; remember the way? And I'll drive back down the trail." Without stopping to see if he agreed, she flew to the pickup. Grinding the gears and spinning the wheels, she turned it around and bumped over the stony surface down the hill.

The family in the house had not seen the children. She gunned the truck back up the hill, and slamming its door as she left it, she stumbled down the path to the river, ignoring the rips to her jeans when she sometimes scooted on her seat.

"Willow," Tyler called softly, "over here." His voice was not urgent, but guarded. "Be quiet."

A rattler, was Willow's first thought. The children were cornered by a rattler. Or a panther. Mitch said that he'd heard the cry of a panther several times. Or even a bear. The wild animals that had been eradicated since Grandma Edna's time were slowly re-establishing themselves in the rougher areas because of the abundance of food from the increase in the deer population.

Trying to be quiet, she half slid and half crawled down the steep path to the river. Almost there, she stopped short and caught her breath. Before her were the two children, perched in the maple tree where on the float trip they had swung out to drop into the river. Tyler was hunched down on the bank with his arms around Barney to hold him and keep him quiet. Grinning, all three pointed across the river to a spot below the gravel bar where they had eaten lunch.

Two grown otters were sliding down the steep muddy bank into the river. Behind them one by one came four smaller otters. Willow watched, fascinated. She could see their little bright eyes and their drooping whiskers. None of their feet were visible as the long brown animals slid down on their chests and bellies and slid gracefully into the water.

Completely oblivious to the group across the river, and probably feeling safe with the expanse of the water protecting them, the otter family was frolicking, nudging one another, splashing, and scampering up the bank to slide down again. Then almost submerged, with just the tops of their heads showing above the water, they swam in playful circles.

In all her time on the river, Willow had never seen otters. She had occasionally spotted their trail and once she and Mitch found a slide which they took to be made by otters, but never the animals themselves. Beavers, muskrats, groundhogs, and even an occasional mink, but never otters. Barney, as interested as the rest, seemed content to watch, probably knowing that he was no match for the adult pair when defending their young. Nobody moved or made a sound until the otters tired of their play and swan leisurely upstream. Something must have startled them, for they all dived out of sight. They did not appear again. Only then did Willow let out her breath.

"Aunt Willow," Dawn said, "did you see them?"

"I never saw otters before," Cory said, climbing out of the tree. "I knew what they were and told Dawn because I have pictures of them in my book at home."

"I never saw them in the wild before, either," Willow said. "They were almost trapped out, and they don't usually come out in the daytime."

Tyler released Barney who started down the river, but changed his mind and returned to Dawn. Tyler then drew Willow down the path to his level. Holding

And Tyler, Too?

her with one hand, he lifted her chin with the finger of his other hand to keep her from avoiding his eyes. With his head tilted and slightly bowed, he looked up at her from under his black eyebrows.

"And you say there's no excitement around here?" He squeezed her hand.

Chapter Eight

When Willow, Tyler, and the children climbed back up the path to the cabin, all talking at once and excited from the glimpse of the wild they had just witnessed, they saw another pickup parked beside Jerry's Chevy on the rock slabs.

"I thought you said no one ever comes here," Tyler said in alarm, stepping in front of her and pushing her back out of sight.

Willow laughed at his precaution. "Tyler, this isn't New York. Nobody's going to mug us."

The children had already climbed from the bluff path and were running on the rock outcropping toward the cabin. "It's Mitch," Cory called back.

Willow couldn't help grinning at Tyler with an I-told-you-so air. His face made a quick change from worried precaution to embarrassment. Even while enjoying her advantage over him, she was surprised at her reaction. Though Tyler's sudden move had momentarily startled her, instead of being annoyed, she was touched. His intentions were good; he was protecting her. But protecting her from Mitch! She chuckled at the thought of Mitch being dangerous.

"Sorry," he said, his face red as he stepped out of her way. "I didn't . . ."

"That's okay, Tyler." She had trouble controlling her giggles. Then she touched his arm and said with sincerity, "I'm sorry I laughed at you. I think that's the first time anyone ever actually stood between me and danger." But thinking of gentle, teddy-bear Mitch as a threat sent her off again. "I can't help it," she tried to apologize.

"I wasn't thinking," Tyler said. "Just an automatic reaction. I guess since we didn't see anyone else during the two days on the river and no one today after we left the highway except the renters at the farmhouse, I was just sort of surprised and on edge to see another car so suddenly." He swept his eyes over the view below them, as he had several times, as if to prove to himself that all that uninhabited space was real. "I've never been anyplace where there were so few people. Nobody to be seen or heard in any direction. That in itself is kind of spooky, and then for a strange car to suddenly appear!" He shook his head in wonder.

"Yeah. After the city it was a natural reaction, I guess." Thinking about it, Willow realized that in the city she was constantly surrounded by people, rarely ever without seeing or hearing someone. She remembered a science fiction movie she'd seen about a future time when the population was so dense that people hardly had room to move. Everyone was literally pressed against other people at all times. She shuddered at that future possibility. Though New York City was not crowded to that extent—the masses of humanity still seemed exciting to her—her living there gave her greater appreciation for her native area. She didn't realize how different it was, accustomed as she was to it, until she watched the wonder of it grow in Tyler's eyes.

These serious thoughts stopped her laughter, but she grinned mischievously and said, "After you, Sir Hugh of the Otters."

"No," Tyler insisted, his face serious. Then a sly smile deepened the cleft in his chin as he swept off his hat, made a deep bow from the waist, and brushing aside the oak limbs hanging over the path, swept his right arm out to point the way. "After you, my damsel in distress." His royal bearing was marred when he almost lost his balance on the steep path.

They both laughed so much that Tyler's left foot slipped on the loose pebbles. He would have fallen had Willow not thrown her arms around him to steady him. She did not immediately release him as they stood in the narrow path, holding on to each other convulsed with laughter.

"Truce?" Tyler asked when he could speak. The sun streaking through the oak trees flashed off a small silver pendant around his neck.

"Truce."

"The kids said you saw some otters," Mitch said. He was standing on top of the bluff just above them. "Pretty rare sight, I admit." From seeing his satisfied smirk, Willow couldn't tell if the otters or she and Tyler holding on to each other were the rare sight.

"He thinks . . ." Willow whispered to Tyler.

"Yeah. Let's don't disillusion him." Tyler winked at her and then kissed her cheek.

And Tyler, Too? 87

Had they been alone, Willow would have quickly put Tyler in his place. The nerve of him! But with Mitch and the kids watching and grinning, she let it go. Looking for something to get their attention away from her and Tyler, she looked beyond them to Mitch's pickup. His truck bed was rounded over with wooden shingles. "Hey," she called, abruptly leaving Tyler and running to inspect the shingles, "you really meant it about restoring the cabin?" In her delight she forgot her embarrassment.

"Of course." He looked from her to Tyler as if trying to figure out what the scene he had just seen meant. When neither offered any explanation, he said, "I had the cabin in mind when I bought these shingles. Just needed the impetus to do something about them. Are you guys game to putting on a new roof?" His question included the children.

"Yeah!" Cory and Dawn both said.

"Sure," Tyler said. "I'd love to."

"Well, that settles it then." Mitch didn't wait for Willow to answer. He, Tyler, and the children went to the truck. Mitch's left arm was on Tyler's shoulder while his right hand was gesturing to the cabin as he explained his plan. The four made a compact group. Cory was beside Mitch and Dawn was holding Tyler's left hand.

Willow didn't move. Her laughing mood was gone, for nothing was funny anymore. Ever since she arrived home, someone else had been directing her actions as if everything that happened had been carefully scripted. Everyone knew what part to play except Willow. The warm feeling from Tyler's arms holding her as they laughed together faded with her rising resentment at Mitch, the kids, everyone. She forgot her fleeting sensation of being protected. For eight years now she had been completely on her own in the greatest city in the world. She, a kid from Hickland. She almost said Smallville, but decided Hickland was more descriptive. During that time she had made every decision. She had plotted out her life and arrived where she wanted to be with the job she wanted in the heart of the nation's garment industry. And she had even greater plans for the future.

But back here her family was in league with big-city Tyler to manipulate her. Like she was no more mature than Cory or Dawn. Well, let *them* fix the cabin. Let *him* take center stage with everyone, her parents and the kids.

And now Mitch. Even he deserted her, his attention riveted on Tyler. He picked up a wooden shingle and, turning it over and over, was explaining to Tyler how with a mallet and froe it was split out of a block of wood cut from the forest.

Willow had had enough. She started toward her father's pickup to go home. They could do it without her, and Mitch could bring them home. Then she stopped. Why punish herself? She wanted to work on this cabin as much as anyone. As children she and Mitch used to plan what they would do to it when they grew up and had the means and the time. Now they were grown, and she had free time. This cabin belonged to *her* ancestors, after all. Mitch, the children, her parents, her brothers—they were her family. The most precious people in her world. And this was her one vacation in a long time—three weeks, a length of time unprecedented in the garment industry.

What was really bothering her? Tyler, of course. He had asked her for a truce and then he ruined it all by kissing her. She could still feel the pressure of his lips on her cheek. Another time and place, and away from Mitch's gleeful eyes, she might have enjoyed it. *Admit it, you did enjoy it, damsel in distress.* Then she smiled and her mood brightened. She pretended to get something from her purse in her father's pickup to cover why she was not with the others. They were carrying armloads of the aromatic cedar shingles to the cabin.

When she joined them, Dawn and Cory immediately danced around her. "Mitch said we can help if you say it's okay. Can we, Aunt Willow? Can we?" Cory begged.

"Will you teach me to hammer real nails?" Dawn asked.

"Willow, do you think we ought to take off the entire roof, including the sheathing, down to the original rafters?" Mitch asked.

Tyler's face looked more youthful than she'd ever seen it. His whole body radiated a new exuberance and purpose. "This is great, Willow," he said, "really great. Would you mind if I did some sketches of the process? Imagine, being allowed to put hand-hewn cedar shingles on a house a hundred and forty years old." He shook his head with the wonder of it all. "And out here in one of the most isolated and perfect spots I've ever seen." Without waiting for her to respond to his question or comments, he hugged her quickly and gathered up another armload of shingles. "I feel like a pioneer. I already smell like one," he said happily, holding his bare arm to his nose. The cedar aroma was mixed with perspiration.

Willow stood beside Mitch's pickup, her foot on the back bumper as her hand rested on the flange of the bed. "You think your folks will mind us doing this?" Mitch asked when he returned for another load. "Or Charley and Gene?" Not waiting for the answer which he knew already, he started toward the cabin. Then he stopped and turned back, aware for the first time that she was not participating in the general activity. A puzzled expression came over his face and he took a couple of steps back to her. He peered at her over his bundle of shingles. "This is all right with you, isn't it?"

"Of course. It's more than all right. It's great." She grabbed a shingle. Not watching what she was doing, she got a splinter in her thumb. Ignoring the prickling pain, she gathered up a few loose shingles and joined Mitch. "We can probably get this roof done in two or three days, or anyway before I have to go back." She walked beside Mitch as they always used to do, planning and organizing their day together.

"Good. You'll have to be the one to oversee it. I can help some. Maybe you can talk your dad into helping. He's not too keen on it, but your mom sure is."

"Yes, she'll get him to help if he can get away from work, and Mom will see to it that we are fed." They both laughed, knowing Maggie's obsession with feeding everyone.

"Charley and Gene?" Mitch asked.

"Probably some. They're pretty busy now. But Tyler and I can do it."

"He's pretty handy," Mitch said. "He seems to take to everything here like a duck to water."

Willow didn't respond. They dumped their shingles

on the growing pile beside the cabin. Willow looked at the roof and the pile. "I doubt these shingles will be enough."

"No, I don't think so either. I don't know if I'll have time enough to make more before you leave."

"Would you show Tyler? He's quite a craftsman."

"Sure."

"And, Mitch, let me know if you have an auction while we're here. Maybe someone selling out, a widow or widower or an old couple selling their farm and moving to town. I think Tyler would enjoy that."

"And you could maybe pick up some antiques?"

"Yeah, that, too. And I could show off my talented cousin to the urban artist."

Mitch grinned with pleasure at her compliment. "I've done nothing like you and Hugh have, but I do all right." He thought for a moment. "Matter of fact, I do have an auction next week. It'd be perfect. I'll let you know."

Willow smiled. She had retaken control of her life. From now on she, not her family, would write the script for the rest of her vacation.

The children dumped the last load of shingles on the impressive-looking pile just to the right of the cabin door. Willow put her arm over Cory's shoulder. Mitch was telling Dawn how much help she had been. All four of them were leaning toward one another as they admired the pile. For the last fifteen minutes Mitch, Willow, and the children had worked together. Willow and the children told Mitch about finding the letters and their futile search for more information. The family unit felt so natural that no one noticed that Tyler was not with them. When Willow remembered him, she looked around. Seated cross-legged on a low rock at the edge of the bluff across the trail from the cabin, Tyler was busy sketching. When she spotted him, he had just flipped a page over, and twisting his body slightly to the left, looked at the group before him and began another sketch.

"Don't move," he said. "You are perfect just as you are. Go ahead talking." His pencil flew over the page. His head did not move from its tilted angle, but his eyes moved constantly up and then down at his paper.

"Go on talking," he repeated, shading in some background. "Just don't spoil your grouping."

"What does grouping mean?" Dawn asked Willow.

"The way we are standing together here all cozy with the cabin behind us."

"Will the picture show this dirt all over my hands?" Dawn asked. She was trying without success to rub off the sticky sap from the shingles.

"Probably." Willow laughed. When Dawn began to object, she added, "They are good stains, pumpkin. Shows that you really worked." She took Dawn's hands in hers to look at the accumulated grime from not just the shingles but the dusty cabin and the river mud. "These hands are your initiation into the Hill Family Log Cabin Restorers."

Cory stuck out his hands, which were even grimier than Dawn's. "Mine, too."

"Yes, all of us." Her hands and Mitch's were equally soiled, though their faces were not streaked like the children's.

"But Mitch's name isn't Hill," Dawn said.

"Or Tyler's," Cory said.

And Tyler, Too?

"And Barney. He helps, too."

"How does he help?" Cory taunted her.

"He keeps the snakes away," Dawn said.

"That he does," Willow said. "And you're right about the name. We better come up with a better one."

While Tyler sketched rapidly, everyone tried to think of an appropriate name. "What about simply Ozark Renovators?" he suggested.

"Cool," Cory said.

"What does renovators mean?" Dawn asked.

"People who fix things just like new," Tyler said.

"Yeah. That's us. We'll make this cabin like new."

"Okay," Willow said. "Ozark Renovators it is." Everyone agreed. "Now kids, the next thing we need is a sign. When we get back to Gramps's house, I'll spell out the words and you guys can make the sign."

Forgetting that they were supposed to be posing, the children clapped their hands and ran to each other, ready to begin immediately. When Willow tried to get them back, Tyler waved her off. He was finished. "This is just a quick sketch of the details. I'll do a finished one later," he said when everyone crowded around him to look at his drawing pad.

Even the children could feel the force of the sketch. There was satisfaction in all their faces. The foreground of smooth rock slabs, the angles of their bodies leaning toward one another, the softened lines of the log cabin behind them, and the protecting trees over all portrayed a natural harmony.

"See," Dawn said, looking at the lines that represented her, "my hands are dirty."

"So is your face," Cory said, pointing to the face

that Tyler had shaded in with his pencil. Dawn gave Cory a shove. He pushed back.

"That's really good," Mitch said. He wasn't as aware of Tyler's artistic talents as Willow. After all, she had been buying his designs for three years.

"Thanks," Tyler said. "Drawings and paintings are my real love. I like the designs I do and the other commercial work also, and they pay well, but drawing like this"—once again he waved his arm to indicate the area—"is pure enjoyment."

"I can see that," Mitch said, looking at Tyler's contented expression.

"For a long time I've wanted to do a unified series, but I could never decide on a subject. I'd start, but then I'd lose interest. Not really inspired. I think that I've found my topic."

"The Ozarks?" Mitch guessed.

"Well, yes, but that is too big, too general. I've been thinking about it. At first I thought of just the scenery. But that wouldn't do. There's lots of scenery everywhere, some much more dramatic than here." He looked over the rounded blue hills. "This scene has appeal, all right, but not enough by itself." He tapped the eraser end of his pencil on the sketch he had just finished. "With this picture, I think I've found my theme."

Mitch and Willow looked at the sketch again, and then at Tyler.

"And what is it?" Willow asked. "Something about people, history, work, family?"

"Yes, exactly." Tyler's face beamed with pleasure that she had caught the essence. "It won't be the Ozarks per se, but this seems to be a more or less untouched area that shows the best of American endeavor and ideals. In Europe you can see scenes similar to this"—he pointed to the old cabin—"but you don't see in the people there the vigor, the hope..." He paused while searching for the words he wanted. "... the ... I guess the best I can do is say, the opportunity and freedom to live up to humanity's potentials and do it in harmony with nature."

"Wow," Cory said. He was impressed, though he couldn't understand all that Tyler was saying.

"What does 'per se' mean?" Dawn whispered. She was trying to follow the conversation but kept getting stuck on unfamiliar words.

"By itself," Willow said. "He means he won't be drawing only about the Ozarks, but about something even more important."

"Like us having fun fixing up things together?" Cory asked.

"Yes. And that is what the whole world should be doing," Tyler said.

"Cool!"

Willow's eyes were full of tears. The depths to Tyler were constantly surprising her. How did a kid from Manhattan gain all this wisdom? Then she realized she was being as prejudiced against him as many New Yorkers had been about her. In spite of his urban sophistication, he was more tolerant and perceptive than she. The message of his drawing said that all people, no matter where they come from, are important.

"I think that's wonderful, Hugh."

Tyler grinned, not only for her compliment but because this was the first time she had used his first name. And she did it unconsciously.

"Maybe you should draw instead of helping us restore this cabin."

"No way," he said. "I'll have enough time to draw all I want. What I need is to experience everything firsthand. I don't think I could have captured the feeling you sense in this sketch if I hadn't spent the afternoon working myself."

As they gathered up their tools and closed the cabin door behind them, ready to leave, Willow taunted Tyler. "So accepting my parents' invitation out here was just an opportunity to visit the Ozarks firsthand?"

"That did enter into it." He tilted his head to look up to her. His black mustache quivered as he tried to keep from grinning.

"You're hopeless," Willow said. She was surprised that she was disappointed. Being pursued had its appeal. It made her feel feminine and wanted.

Tyler looked ahead to see that Mitch was climbing into his truck and the kids were chasing each other behind Jerry's truck as they played tag with Barney. "But that wasn't the main reason I came." He put his pad in his backpack and swung it over his shoulder to free his right hand.

Willow felt a lift inside her. "No? What was it?"

"I wanted to rescue a damsel in distress." He leaned over and with the forefinger of his free hand under her chin, tilted it up to face him. Then he gave her another quick kiss, this time on her lips. He hurried around to the passenger's side of the pickup before she could react.

Willow stood alone in front of the closed-up cabin, a crowbar in one hand and a hammer in the other, her emotions completely out of control. But, she had to admit, she enjoyed the kiss.

Chapter Nine

The next few days flew by. Willow, Tyler, and the children drove out to the farm early every day before it got hot to work on the Dawson cabin roof. Jerry, Mitch, and the brothers had spent a day tearing off the metal roof and the old wooden shingles under it. Most of the sheathing boards were in bad condition, so they replaced them. Then the men turned the job over to the Ozark Renovators.

Since everyone was having so much fun, and to teach the children responsibility and business sense, Willow suggested they "incorporate." She printed up some certificates on Maggie's computer. The children's mothers declined, but Charley, Gene, Maggie, and Jerry, in addition to the original renovators, were delighted to "buy" shares. Ownership of each share would be earned by an hour of labor.

The shareholders had a meeting to elect the board of directors and officers. They unanimously voted in as directors Willow, Mitch, Cory, Dawn, and Tyler. Willow was president, Tyler vice-president, and Mitch secretary-treasurer.

The directors soon developed a system of working—Willow and Tyler on the roof to nail down the shingles, Cory and Dawn to keep them supplied with shingles and nails, and to retrieve their hammers when they dropped them. When they had placed enough shingles on the lower roof edge to give a place to sit, Willow let each child place and nail down a few shingles while she stood behind them on the ladder. The slant of the roof was not great, and the kids soon climbed all over it like monkeys, their sneakers gripping the rough shingles.

Since the children were slow and some of their work had to be redone when they weren't looking, Willow hoped that nailing shingles for a few minutes would soon become old and they would want to play. She could work much faster by herself. But their staying power was much greater than she imagined. She was the one who had to limit how long they could work, as she insisted on being beside them in case they would slip. Curbing her impatience, she let them learn and share in the renovation.

Since sketching took too much time away from the restoring work, Tyler took quick photographs. He kept his camera either near at hand or strapped over his shoulder as he worked. When he paused to rest, he took photographs. Willow and the children soon paid no attention to his constantly photographing them.

After a lunch and an afternoon swim in the river, the weary group would head home. But Tyler's energy was indefatigable. He spent the remainder of the afternoon at Mitch's house riving shingles. Mitch already had some logs cut and the setup for splitting out the shingles. After a few lessons, Tyler was doing them by himself while Mitch was at his auction barn working or out in the country conducting a sale.

And Tyler, Too?

Understanding wood and how to work with it, Tyler was soon expertly splitting off shingles to the correct slant, thicker at one end than the other. Accustomed to finishing wooden articles by planing and sanding, he enjoyed the rough natural look of the shingles. Splinters of wood clinging to each piece merely enhanced the rustic effect.

Each afternoon, glorying in his work, Tyler brought back the shingles he'd made. The next day, he nailed up those shingles himself. The newer wood was lighter in color than the seasoned ones Mitch had purchased. Tyler scattered the greener shingles among the others, giving the roof a mottled effect. "It won't be long until all the shingles will weather alike."

"I like it like this," Cory said.

"So do I," Tyler said.

On the day when Willow and Tyler nailed the last of the ridge shingles and smeared tar around the chimney to prevent any leaks, Mitch, Maggie, and Jerry were all there to celebrate. When Tyler climbed down the ladder with Willow close behind him, the group on the ground cheered. Before celebrating with Maggie's cake and lemonade, they took their usual swim to wash and cool off while Jerry and Maggie cleaned up the rest of the old boards and roofing around the cabin.

When the cheerful group climbed the steep path from the river and Maggie set out the refreshments on the big rock slab, they marveled at how improved the cabin was with the new roof. The windows were still boarded up, there were still gaps in the chinking between the logs big enough to stick a fist through, several foundation stones were missing, and the front door still sagged. But like a cowboy with a new Stetson hat, the cabin seemed to stand taller.

"Shows up all the other things we need to do to it," Maggie said.

"They can wait," Jerry said. "The roof was the main thing." He put his arm around his wife. "That roof will last another hundred years." Then turning to Tyler, "Did you know that some of those old shingles we tore off were the original ones?"

"Really?"

"Yep. Made right and cared for, wooden shingles will last a long time. Of course, if we hadn't put that metal roof on over them thirty years ago, this cabin would be just a pile of rotted logs now." Jerry patted Willow on the back. "Good job, Willow." Then he held out his arms for his grandchildren. They ran to him. "And you two, you worked as hard as anyone. I'm very proud of you. That roof will be there for you to tell your grandchildren that you put it on."

"And we can tell them all about Grandma Edna and Grandpa Ben," Dawn said, hugging him.

During the past week everyone had been so busy working on and thinking about the roof that only Maggie kept looking for more information about the Union payroll. Willow and Tyler never resumed searching inside in the cabin wall the day that they were interrupted by the disappearance of the children. They had already decided that there couldn't be anything hidden behind the walling. All they were doing was damaging the cabin. On the last day, while the others were finishing the roof, Maggie had walked around inside and out searching for the umpteenth time to see if she had missed anything.

"How much time did Grandpa Ben have to hide the payroll, do you think?" Maggie asked as she took a big bite of her white cake with chocolate fudge icing. Everyone was seated or standing on the biggest slab, which they always used as a table, though it was only six inches higher than the others around it.

Willow almost choked on the lemonade she was swallowing at her mother's abrupt change of subject. But that was like her mother. Finish one project and get right on to the next—especially if the next one was an unfinished one.

"Well, let's see. According to the story, he heard the news at the store. Five miles over there." Willow pointed up the rocky trail over the ridge toward the old ford. "Dad, how long would it take them to get back on horseback?"

"If he galloped, which he undoubtedly did where the trail would let him, about half an hour, I'd say. There's pretty rough going with all the hills and crossing the river. Many places he'd have to walk his horse."

"Okay, then when he got back home he had to take the horse or mule that was carrying the money someplace to hide it."

"We wouldn't know how long that took since we don't know where he hid it," Mitch said.

"Yes, but let's see what else he did."

"He laid a false trail," Maggie said, "so the Rebels wouldn't come by the cabin."

"How do you suppose he did that?" Willow asked.

Everyone was silent for a few moments. Jerry said, "We can assume that the Rebels were coming up from the south, and since the store was south of the cabin,

I'd wager that he cut back to the store with his whole detail and headed east over that old Rolla trail to cross the river south of here. That way the Rebels wouldn't use our ford or come by the cabin."

"But that would have been very risky," Mitch said. "He put himself and his men in danger. He headed right into the path of the Confederate soldiers."

"But it protected Grandma Edna and the baby," Maggie said.

"And the payroll," Willow added. "I bet that was part of his reasoning."

"And the money was safer wherever he hid it than taking it with him," Mitch said.

When no one said anything else, Willow asked, "Besides going back to the store, does anyone have any other thoughts about what he might have done to lay a false trail?"

"I agree with Jerry," Tyler said, joining in the discussion for the first time, though he had been listening intently. "If he hightailed it straight east from here back to Rolla and St. Louis, the Southern soldiers would follow the main road, which would lead them right here to his wife. He knew the danger that would put her in. So in order to avoid that, it seems to me that he had no choice but to go back to the store. Unless there was another route. Was there any other trail between here and the store leading east?"

"No," Jerry, Mitch, and Maggie all said.

"Okay, then," Willow said, "let's assume that he went back to the store to the old Rolla road leading east. And the people at the store would see his unit. Besides the obvious trail he would have left, the Rebels

And Tyler, Too?

could have forced the people at the store to tell them which way they went. Do you agree?"

Everyone did. "Some of the people might have sympathized with the Rebels," Jerry said. "They may have sent word somehow to them that Ben was here in the first place. You know the country was divided in loyalties."

"Okay. Then he went back to the store. That took another half hour."

"So far there's a whole hour just riding," Mitch said. "We don't know how much ahead of the army the rider was who warned him at the store, but he couldn't have been too far ahead."

"A single rider who knows the land can go faster than an army," Jerry said.

"But it probably wasn't a whole army," Maggie said.

"No, but even if it were only a few men, with supplies and stuff, they couldn't go as fast as a single rider," Jerry insisted.

"The upshot of it seems to be that Grandpa Ben didn't have much time," Willow said. "The very fact that he was overtaken and killed would indicate that. If the Rebels were a long time coming, he would have gotten away."

"I'd say that when he got to the cabin from the store, he didn't have more than a few minutes to hide the money," Jerry said. "Half hour at most."

Willow looked around at the group. "Surely not more than that," Mitch agreed.

Maggie stood up. "And to get the money, take it to the hiding place, hide it, remove any trace, and get back to the cabin, all within a half hour?" She held out her hands and turned completely around, encompassing the area surrounding the cabin. "It can't be on the river. It can't be as far as the old ford." She sat down, discouraged. "It's got to be right here, very close. But it isn't. In all these years too many people have looked, and it's just not here."

Nobody said anything. Maggie was the one who held on tenaciously to the reality of the money. Reason had convinced her to give it up years ago, but Dawn finding the letters reignited her zeal.

"Maybe he hid it on the march somewhere between here and the store, or afterward," Jerry said. "Edna doesn't say in her note that he for sure hid it, did she?"

Willow pulled out of her pocket a copy of Grandma Edna's note. She read, " 'He didn't say nothing to me about what he was doing that morning afore he left in such a hurry, but I thought then and still do now that he did something with the payroll.' "

"See?" Jerry said. "No real proof it is around here."

"But obviously he was doing something. Grandma Edna said so," Maggie said.

"It could have been anything."

"Maybe he was getting rid of any signs around the place that he had been there," Tyler said.

"Yes," Jerry said. "Or hiding the supplies he bought at the store. He could have done other things."

"But why would Grandma Edna think it had to do with the money?" Maggie said. "She thought so strongly that she wrote it down on a piece of paper and put it with his letters. And she saved it all those years."

"Maybe she thought it for the same reason that you and all the others of her descendants do, because it is romantic and intriguing." Jerry raised his right eyebrow and winked at Maggie. "It's a good story. Everyone gets hooked on treasure hunts."

He looked around at the group. His words did not convince anyone. The others, like Maggie, had renewed hope after finding the letters.

"Well, anyway," Jerry said, taking Maggie's hand in his, "we've had fun looking for it. Willow, Tyler, and the kids have had some excitement. It's a great story and heritage to leave your grandkids."

"I've never heard a better one," Tyler said. "I think it's incredible."

"I know you're right, Tyler," Maggie said, patting his hand. "I'm very glad that you came to help us restore our old cabin. We wouldn't have found the letters or done anything to the cabin without your interest."

"I didn't do anything."

"Your wanting to see the cabin and hear the story of Grandma Edna started it all," Willow said. "All of us, even the kids, are looking at the old family legend with different eyes. Yes, Mom's right, Tyler. We wouldn't have done anything without you."

Willow was surprised at herself. She truly meant what she said. And just a week ago she was bemoaning that this New York artist had ruined her long-awaited vacation. As she looked back on the first week of it, she knew it had been one of the best times she'd had since her free childhood days with Mitch. Better. Now she was an adult with grown-up feelings. She smiled at Tyler. Her heart skipped a beat when he lifted his eyebrows and smiled at her.

He then pulled out his sketch pad, backed up a few steps, and started sketching the group. Maggie and Jerry were additions to this group scene from the one he'd done the first day. Seated around the slightly raised slab in the old roadway, the family was in a semicircle with their backs to the cabin. On the rough rock surface were the remains of the cake with the knife still on the platter, a thermos of drink, and scattered paper cups. Dawn was sitting in Jerry's lap. Cory and Willow were chatting with Maggie, while Mitch and Jerry were talking and gesturing with their hands full of layer cake. Behind them the new roof of the old cabin under the late-afternoon sunlight was like a beacon shining on the family. Tyler's newer shingles reflected pinpoints of light.

"Maggie," Tyler said when he showed her the sketch, "I can't think of any greater richness than you already have."

Maggie studied the picture showing the family accord and then at the real people around her. She smiled as she handed it back to him. "You're right, Tyler. I couldn't ask for more."

Willow still held her copy of Grandma Edna's note. "Richness," she repeated.

"What?"

"Tyler just said richness. That is the word that Grandpa Ben used." She read from the note, " 'I want you to find comfort in the richness of our love.' "

"Exactly the same meaning that I meant," Tyler said.

"But maybe he said richness to mean the payroll.

And Tyler, Too?

He also says, 'Wherever I travel on the road of life, I will treasure you.' He uses treasure, not 'hold you in my heart,' or 'I'll always think of you.' "

Maggie stood up and stated as definite, "He meant the payroll money. And it is around here very close."

"I think so, too," Willow said. The children, Mitch, and Tyler nodded. Only Jerry, the realist, was unconvinced.

"Come on, kids," Maggie said, "let's put this stuff back in the car." When they stepped onto the rock slab to gather up the food, it teetered just slightly with their weight.

"I better fix that slab again," Jerry said. Glad of something to change the subject, he turned to Tyler to explain. "See here, the water runs down this old trail when it comes a big rain like we had just before you came. In ages past it washed away the topsoil, exposing these rocks. They are pretty resistant, but old Mother Nature is still trying to level this ridge. The runoff washes out the road and keeps working on these slabs here, carrying away what gravel and dirt is around them. Every so often I have to bring in a load of gravel to stabilize them so we can drive over them."

"I'll do it for you," Tyler said. "Now that the roof is finished, I need another project. I'll buy a load of gravel in town and . . ."

Everyone laughed at him. Puzzled, he looked to Willow to explain what he said that was so funny.

"With a river on our land full of gravel bars, we never have to buy gravel. It's there for the taking."

"But," Mitch said, grinning, "you'll have to shovel it into the truck yourself."

"It'll build up your back and arm muscles," Jerry said.

"And then shovel it out again up here," Mitch added. "Still game?"

"Sure. That'd be great," Tyler said.

Jerry took his arm. "Come over here and I'll show you. . . ." The two men walked over to Jerry's pickup.

Maggie smiled when Willow kept watching Tyler. Willow's face was happier than it had been for a long time. "Thank you, Grandma Edna, for the richness you have brought to our lives," she said aloud.

"What'd you say, Mom?" Willow said, pulling her attention from Tyler.

"Nothing, dear. Just mumbling."

But Willow had heard what her mother had said, and she guessed correctly the reason for her mother's smug expression. It was the one she always wore when she finally got what she wanted. And Willow also knew from Maggie's quick glance from Tyler to her own smiling face what she was pleased about.

"Well, okay, Mom. You win. I'm glad you invited him here, but that's all. Now don't you go planning anything more. Promise?"

"I promise," Maggie said, and then aside to Mitch whispered, "No need for me to do anything more."

Mitch grinned and nodded agreement because he knew more than his aunt did. Not a tattletale, he hadn't told anyone about seeing Willow and Tyler in each other's arms on the trail the day he brought the shingles, or the stolen kiss in front of the cabin that they didn't think anyone saw.

Chapter Ten

A few days later Willow and Tyler were alone in her dad's pickup driving to a farm in the north part of the county where Mitch was crying a sale. True to his word, Mitch told Willow of this auction—an old couple selling out and moving into a retirement complex. Almost everything was for sale—stock, machinery, and household goods.

This was the first time they had been alone. When Tyler first came, Willow had insisted on the children's company. At home there was always Maggie and often Jerry, even after the children went home. Willow didn't know how to behave or what to talk about with no audience. The business reserve she had always maintained with him had broken down from their two weeks of sharing and working together.

The sale would be a good conversation topic, Willow decided. "I think you will really enjoy this. All of the couple's neighbors will be there, plus half the county. Auction sales are social gatherings. Of course, there is much serious buying—there'll probably be out-of-county stockmen and farmers as well as some antique hunters. But there will also be many people there just out of curiosity to see what's for sale and who else is there. Everyone has a good time."

"I'm looking forward to it," Tyler said. As Willow sped along the highway, he was taking in the scenery along the road. When they passed a field of corn or soybeans, he watched the tractor and cultivator crawl through the rows as long as he could see them. But most of the view from the highway was either small hay fields and pastures with cattle and horses or deep woods.

"Beautiful country," he said. "It's so varied. Never monotonous. The expanse of fields give relief to the thick forests. And the houses and barns contrast with the wildness of the bluffs and rivers."

Neither said anything for a few miles. Willow was surprised that she was comfortable with the silence. She didn't feel the need to make conversation.

"Look!" Tyler said, excitedly pointing to his right. "Isn't that a wild turkey?"

Willow slowed down. In a hollow clearing was a single tom turkey. He did not fly, but ran from the small, recently mowed hay field where he had been feeding into the brush cover at the edge of the timber encircling the field.

Tyler grabbed his sketch pad from his ever-present backpack and drew some rapid lines on a sheet. "Incredible!"

Willow put out her right hand to touch his bare arm. "I'm really glad you like it, Hugh."

Tyler stopped sketching to put his hand over Willow's. He held it a moment until she needed it to make a turn. "I love to hear you use my first name."

That was such an unexpected reply that she didn't

know what to say. In fact, she didn't realize that she was using his first name. "Well, I got used to hearing my family call you Tyler, but now it seems too . . ." She didn't know just what she meant. ". . . too distant now." She was embarrassed. Switching unconsciously to his first name revealed to both of them some major shift in her feelings toward him. Until she knew what she felt, she was trying to keep to herself her growing attraction for him. Even her lame reason showed that they had long passed being only business associates. To cover herself she said, "And the name Hugh somehow didn't seem to fit you."

"Oh?"

"Not at first," she quickly said when she sensed disappointment in his voice. "But now it does."

"How come?" He wasn't going to let her get off too easily. A quick glance at him showed he wasn't disappointed. He was grinning as if he knew something funny that she didn't.

Glad that she hadn't offended him, she said, "You're different here. In New York you are very much the modish big-city artiste—your clothes, hairstyle, jewelry." She laughed and continued, "I know that it's part of your professional persona, like mine is efficiency, take-charge attitude, makeup, dresses, hose, heels—all the nonsense you have to put up with in the business world. It's really just requirements for the job. You and me both. And I didn't look beyond that facade."

"And now?"

She let out her breath before she answered and gripped the steering wheel as she stared straight ahead down the road. She put on her signal light and zipped around a slow-moving farm truck before she answered. "Now, I see that you are a much more complicated person." Though she didn't look at him, she knew he was grinning. "You retain the sensitivity of an artist, but you have many other qualities also that continually surprise me."

"For instance?" Hugh's voice was lighthearted, almost daring her. He was greatly enjoying this. He shot a quizzical glance at her, and continued to look out the windows.

"You'll get swell-headed if I keep on."

"No, I won't. I pretty well know myself. I'm interested in what you've learned of me."

"Oh, for one, you are darn sure of yourself, just like now." They both laughed.

Willow was about to change the subject to something safer, like the scenery, when he asked, "So how come the name Hugh suits me now?"

This was a safer subject. She relaxed her fingers that were clamped on the wheel. "Well, I'm into names. Sort of a hobby. They fascinate me, maybe because I have such an unusual name myself. Have you noticed that most of the time names really fit the person? Not mine, of course, but others do. American Indians wait to give names until the person earns the name. With us, how do parents know even before a child is born what they will be like? Maybe the person grows to fit the name, do you think?" Without waiting for an answer, she said, "Take my mother. Could she be anything other than a Maggie?"

Hugh laughed. "She could never be a Celeste."

"Or a Priscilla." They both shook their heads and

chuckled. "See what I mean? Maybe she had to grow into being a Maggie."

"But you didn't grow into a Willow," Hugh said seriously, looking at her. "You were born Willow."

"Ugh!" After a few seconds she said, "I never used to like my name, and I almost changed it when I moved to New York. But now I guess it's okay. It's different. Have you ever heard of another Willow Hill?"

"No way. There could never be another." Hugh was dead serious. Then he resumed his teasing manner. "But you still haven't told me why you think now that the name Hugh suits me."

"Well, as I said, I am into names. The English language is rich in names and here in America even more so, with so many foreign-language names of immigrants from all over the world." She had the feeling that Hugh already knew this, but once started on a favorite subject she knew much about, she couldn't stop. "The name Hugh is English, French, and Teutonic." Hugh merely nodded as she continued. "Names have meanings to them, too, did you know that?"

"Yes."

"And in all three of those languages Hugh means intelligent. Did you know that?"

"Yes."

"So Hugh does fit you." As she always did, she braked slightly when the road crossed a creek so she could look both ways up and down the stream. "Only somehow it doesn't. I'm used to Hugh now, but I always thought of you as having some other first name."

"Like what?"

"Oh." Now this conversation was getting difficult. She was glad they were almost at the sale. Studying his dark eyes, black hair and mustache, and his whole demeanor exuding Latin charm, she tried to think of an appropriate name. "Something like . . . uh . . . Antonio. Or Jacques. No . . ." She paused. "No, you are more a Miguel."

Hugh jerked his head back to the headrest in surprise. "You are really something. I guess you are right about names fitting the person. What about Miguel Da Costa? Does that name suit me?"

She slowed down to make the turn onto a gravel road. There was a temporary sign at the junction with an arrow and these words: *Mitch Willard, Auctioneer. Auction today.*

"Are you serious?" She couldn't tell.

"Yes. That's the name my parents gave me."

"Aw . . ."

"Truly. I changed it."

"But I thought . . ."

"No, Willow Hill, who no one in all of New York City would guess is from the Ozarks, my background is not what you pegged me, a kid from the streets of Manhattan turned artist. I was born and spent the first nine years of my life in a small village on the northwestern coast of Portugal."

Willow opened her mouth to say something. She was so surprised and had so many questions she couldn't think which one to ask.

Hugh continued, "I didn't speak English until my father brought my mother and me to New York. He was a fisherman in Portugal who ended up with a construction job in the U.S. That allowed him to bring us over. And that was when I became a kid growing up in the streets of lower Manhattan. That part of your assessment of me is correct."

Willow pulled over to the side of the gravel road and stopped. "I had no idea."

"I told you that you knew nothing about me." He was enjoying her embarrassment.

Willow nodded. "Your parents now? Are they still in the United States?"

"Both have died." When Willow showed sympathy, he said, "It was a few years ago. All my relatives are in Portugal and I haven't kept in touch since my parents' deaths." He paused to see her reaction. "Come on, it's all right. I'm not contagious." He smiled at her amazement. "Let's get on to the sale or we'll be late. I want to look around before Mitch starts."

Willow pulled back onto the road. The wheels spun on the loose gravel when she released the clutch too quickly. With a change of mood, Hugh teased, "Now maybe you can understand why I jumped at the chance to be with a close-knit family again."

Not to be outdone, Willow taunted, "So now it's not only the lure of the Ozarks that made you accept Mom and Dad's invitation. It was my family."

"Guilty as charged, but neither reason was the main one, and you know it. I needed to learn about the rest of you, the person under the executive persona, as you called it. Both the Ozarks and your family held the answer to that. I knew there must be a real person in there." He placed his left hand on her denim-covered knee. She laid hers over his and squeezed it before she had to put it back on the wheel to pass an oncoming car on the narrow road.

Neither spoke as she parked among the trucks and cars in the improvised space in a field. They hurried first to the back of Mitch's business van, which was his temporary office and a lunch counter where Amy officiated. She greeted them and gave them their sale numbers. Willow was surprised when Hugh got one for himself. He stuck it into the band of his straw hat. "Never know," he said. "I might see something I want."

They crossed the lawn to where the crowd was gathered in the shade of the huge maple trees around a row of furniture and a long improvised table of planks and sawhorses loaded with household items. Hugh's enthusiasm was infectious. They both behaved like children at a circus as they mingled in the crowd. They touched every item that pleased them. Hugh ran his hands over the smooth patina of an old rocker. Willow smelled the rose potpourri still emanating from the dresser drawers. In the empty house Willow had to hold Hugh to keep him from sliding down the bannister. In the barnyard Hugh climbed up into the cab of the huge tractor. Like a kid he gripped the wheel, moving it as if driving. "Arrooooomm, nummm, nummm," he made boyish noises like Cory did with his toy tractor.

"A perfect example of middle America," Hugh said, photographing the variety of people of all ages. Then pointing his camera at the two-story, white frame house of the early twentieth century with dormer windows and big porches front and back, he added, "Even the buildings. That house is a middle stage between the log cabin and the modern rural homes."

Willow followed him as he circled the house. "Do you suppose your Dawson ancestors would have built a house like this if Ben had survived the war?"

"Probably."

"Would your Grandma Edna have built one if she'd found the payroll?"

Willow didn't have an answer to that. Thinking back to her own mother and the grandmother that she could remember, she tried to imagine what they would have done. And she herself. What would she do in the same situation?

"I don't think so," she finally answered. "Grandma Edna loved her cabin and she could have built on to it in later years even without the payroll money. But she didn't. Maybe it was all that she had left of her dead husband. If we're right in our assumptions of his actions that day, he sacrificed himself to protect her and their home. He undoubtedly knew that the extra time he spent there jeopardized his safety."

She watched a young woman carrying a nine-month-old baby. She was crooning and rocking the baby to keep him quiet. "No, I don't think she would have built a big house, even if she had found the money. I think that she would have given it back to the army. Now, the next generations, I don't know what they would have done."

"Interesting thought," Hugh said. "Let's say hypothetically that you find the money now. Does it belong to the army? Or finders keepers?"

"I don't know. Officially it's listed as confiscated. Also there is no proof, that is, *if* we find it, that it ever belonged to the army. No one can prove it was that payroll. And maybe there is a statute of limitations. We'd have to look into that. But you know, Hugh, for all of us now, for me, my brothers, the kids, Mom, Mitch—and we're the only living descendants—it isn't the money that we really want. That isn't the reason we're so interested."

"What, then," Hugh asked, "if not that?"

"The satisfaction of solving the mystery. Documentation that the family legend is correct. Finding our piece of lost history that ties us into the larger national history. That's the real reason. You see, Hugh, Missouri history doesn't go back too far. Nothing like in Europe, or even in the East. Our family history begins here, five or six generations back. And we are richer than a lot of our neighbors in that we have a bit of oral history handed down to us. We just want to preserve it. Knowing that it really happened will do that."

Hugh shook his head in wonder. "You keep amazing me. I must admit that I didn't know you any better than you knew me. I've uncovered a completely different woman inside the fashion executive of Mansfield and Logan."

"Is that good or bad?" She ran her fingers through her short hair that a beauty salon operator hadn't set since she arrived home. Her face without any makeup looked up into his. Her blouse tail hung out over her worn jeans, whose rolled-up legs brushed her dusty sneakers. She was enjoying this turn in the conversation, as now Hugh was on the spot.

"I like complicated women." He grinned, not the least disconcerted. " 'Cause I'm a complicated guy."

"Yes, you are, Sir Hugh." She laughed. "Sir Hugh

does have a better ring to it than Sir Miguel Da Costa.'' She shook her head. ''No, that won't do at all. Sounds like something from *Don Quixote*. Not you at all.''

''Even if I do go about rescuing damsels in distress from threatening cousins?''

''Even then.'' She laughed. ''You don't fight windmills. You draw them so everyone can see their beauty and function of harnessing nature's power without harming the environment.''

She grabbed his hand. ''Speaking of Mitch, let's go. He's about to start.'' Holding hands, their fingers intertwined, they ran back to the row of furniture in front of the house and the table covered with small household items. Mitch was gathering up the first items he would auction off. When he spotted Willow and Hugh, he put up his hand in greeting.

''All right, folks, gather around and we'll start the sale. Appreciate you all coming out on such a hot day.'' Mitch's voice carried over the lawn, so that those looking at other items heard him and joined the group, standing around him in a semicircle. ''We'll start here at the house with the furniture. Then we'll go over to the lot with the machinery. Last of all at the barn, where we'll sell the stock.'' He explained the sale procedures. ''All rightee, here we go on this rocker.'' He held up for everyone to see the old wooden rocker whose patina Hugh had admired.

''That one's perfect,'' Willow said to Hugh. ''I'm going to bid.''

''This rocker was handmade back in the 1800s. A real Ozark antique. Here we go. Who'll give me ten there? Ten? Let's go. Five? Five-five-five-and-a-half-now-six-now-seven-seven. Let's go, folks. Got lots to sell today."

Even while she was bidding, Willow was admiring Mitch. He was handsome, dressed in western attire—bolo tie over a white western shirt, pressed jeans over black tooled boots, and a gray felt hat with a pinch crease and rolled brim. His musical chant continued, coaxing bids from the audience. After he got Willow's bid, he turned to a bearded man on his left who was bidding against her and bombarded him with his chant until he nodded. Then back to Willow and with her bid back to the bearded man.

"I hate to buy the first thing in the sale, but I want that chair," Willow said to Hugh while Mitch was trying to elicit another nod from the bearded man.

Hugh had been observing everything. "Mitch started on it first on purpose because he figured you'd want it. At a sale bidding usually starts slow, so this way you can get it at a good price."

When Willow looked at him in wonder that he knew so much about sales, he laughed. "I've been to auctions. Not like this, not a farm auction, but lots of art auctions. The principle is the same."

Mitch was trying to raise Willow's last bid of eighteen dollars. ". . . now nineteen-nineteen-go-nineteen-go-nineteen." When he got that bid, he turned to Willow. "Twenty-twenty-now-twenty." Willow nodded. Without pausing in his chant, Mitch addressed the bearded man. "And-a-half-twenty-and-a-half-twenty-and-a-half-twenty-and-a-half last chance." He paused. His blue eyes darted quickly over the crowd. When there were no more bids, "Sold! The rocker to number thirty, Willow Hill, for twenty dollars. Con-

And Tyler, Too?

gratulations, Willow, you got a bargain.'' He was grinning as much as she.

Willow clapped her hands in delight. Hugh hugged her and swung her around, almost bumping into the women behind them. Ignoring everyone, he kissed her cheek in congratulations on her purchase. Though moving to the next item, Mitch watched Willow with Hugh. "Okay folks, here is a good dresser...."

At the end of the sale, as Willow and Hugh drove back to town, an old-fashioned wooden cupboard called a safe, a hickory-bottomed stool, and a homemade wood plane that Hugh couldn't resist bidding on kept company with the rocker in the pickup bed. Willow was more excited with her few purchases than if she had landed a big clothing order for her latest line. The total experience—the friendliness of the people, eating hot dogs and candy bars washed down by sodas, Hugh's eagerness, her pride in Mitch and the business he had built from nothing, and the childlike lightness within her—made her feel as if she were floating rather than bumping down the gravel road to the highway. She was smelling roses and lilacs rather than the yellow dust from the stream of cars ahead of her leaving the sale.

A perfect day. She didn't even notice the smarting of her face and bare arms unprotected from the sun. Her face was dry and her hair tousled from the wind that had blown most of the day. She didn't care.

The day was reminiscent of the times she and Mitch used to go to sales in all parts of the county when they were in high school. No wonder he was so good at it. Maybe those excursions also sparked her interest in sales and merchandising. Both of them learned techniques and what people would spend money for. Funny, she hadn't thought about those early years and what she and Mitch did together as background for her own success in quite a different field from his.

As if Hugh knew what she was thinking, he said, "Mitch is very good, isn't he? He handled that crowd masterfully and got better bids than most of the stuff was worth."

"Yes, except what I bought. Did you notice that he cut off the bidding at what he thought the stuff I bought was worth? He knew I'd bid on up, but he stopped it with my bid."

"Yeah, I noticed, but I don't think anyone else did."

"We got some great antiques today."

"We sure did. Do you have any idea what that stuff would bring in the East?"

"Yes, I do. That rocker I bought for twenty dollars would be about a hundred."

"Or more."

"I've been thinking that these things plus the table, bedstead, and the other stuff still in the cabin and what Mitch has already collected will about refurnish it," Willow said.

"Now what we need to do is refinish some of those pieces. We can . . ."

While Hugh was outlining what they could do, Willow was thinking of Mitch. Their friendship was very special to her. He was more a brother than either Charley or Gene, though they were dear to her. She and Mitch had had a sort of telepathic oneness when they were kids. The main reason she was so upset when Hugh showed up at the family gathering was that he would intrude on her time with her cousin. She wondered if she had been comparing every man she met with Mitch. Few could match him.

But during this visit she learned she could have that comradeship with someone else and, in addition, feel much more than brotherly love. Hugh had not only measured up to Mitch, but had qualities Mitch lacked. He could elicit feelings that no cousin could.

"... I was wondering if they would mind?" Hugh poked her to get her attention. "Hugh to Willow, come in. Are you there?"

"Oh, Hugh, I'm sorry. I was thinking back over today, how wonderful it was and how glad I am that you are here. What were you saying?"

"That I wonder if your parents would let me bunk in the cabin for a few weeks after you go back. I could pay for my rent by fixing the doors and windows. It would be an ideal place for me to work on my new series."

Chapter Eleven

"I can't imagine why you would want to stay in the old Dawson cabin," Willow said to Hugh. Since he first suggested it the day of the auction, she couldn't fathom what possessed him, or why her parents cheerfully agreed. Keen as she was on reading and learning all she could about pioneer living, she never for once wanted to experience it.

"It'll be exciting."

"I can't see anything exciting about doing without electricity."

"Your mother's kerosene lamps are just fine. They will give the kind of light I'll need for my drawings. I don't plan to do much reading at night anyway."

"But pumping water out of that old well. Hugh, it may not work or the water may not be good. No one has used the pump in years."

"It's all right. I checked it. The pump works and the water is clear and pure. I won't need much, as I'll have the whole river to bathe in."

Willow's vacation was about over. She and Hugh were enjoying a short river float down to the cabin. Mitch had brought them and his canoe to the put-in place. After attending to some business, he planned to

And Tyler, Too?

pick them up at the access point at the old ford. Afterward he would drive them to the cabin around the road across the highway bridge. He had in his pickup shell Willow's auction purchases and the camping equipment Hugh would need.

Since Willow and Hugh were drifting lazily in a quiet eddy, Willow held her paddle close, moving it slightly as needed to keep the canoe pointed in the right direction. They were in no hurry on this sultry, hot, overcast day in July, content to float with the natural current.

"But the cabin probably still leaks," she said.

"No, it doesn't. I checked that also after that big rain we had the other day. Some water blew in the cracks between the logs and some came in under the door. I can easily fix that. The roof held."

Since Willow knew that he had made up his mind and would have an answer for any other objections she would have, she didn't try anymore.

"Don't worry so much, Willow. I'm looking forward to it. It's a great opportunity. I'll experience what it was like to live like your ancestors did. I can then understand more the character of the people who live here now. Maybe I can put some of that feeling into my paintings."

Since the recent rain, the river was about a foot higher than the first float they made. And murkier, a chalky green. The current, even in the quiet eddies, carried them along at almost the speed of someone walking along the bank. The riffles were more fun, for the greater water flow that was still constricted to the narrow chutes rolled and bubbled its way through. Though there were whitecaps on the water, the two paddlers skillfully held the canoe to the crest of the current, avoiding boulders, logs, and accumulated trash recently dumped in unexpected places by the higher water.

When they cleared the fastest riffle they had yet run, Hugh said, "That's coming close to the way it was in the skiff out in the ocean when my father and I used to go fishing off our village in Portugal."

"Tell me about it."

"There's not much to tell. I was little. Dad did all the work. Most of the time he wouldn't let me go, but if the ocean was calm, he sometimes took me. Being in a boat again makes me remember it. You feel so masterful controlling a small boat in the water. It's different from driving a car. There the road is stationary. It's just your skill on a solid surface. On the ocean, and here on this river, you're in a constantly moving and changing plane that has its own ideas of where you're going. It's been a long time since I've thought of those times in Portugal."

"Were they good memories?"

"Yes." He paused and then said, "And no. We were very poor. Individual fishermen with their skiffs couldn't compete with the big trawlers. Got so my father had to go farther out to get his catch. So it was great for us when he landed the job in the United States."

"How did you feel about coming to America?"

"Oh, for me it was unending excitement and novelty. I liked the city, my school, and the friends I soon made. But my mother had a hard time. She missed her family, but because it was so much better for Dad and me, she never complained."

"Did you ever go back?"

"Oh yes, to visit every other year or so. Mom liked that."

"Did she want to move back?" Willow asked.

"Not really. Not after a while. Much easier for her here. She got a job, too. We did all right."

"What about you? Would you ever want to go back to live there?"

He turned back to look at her. "No way. Best thing Dad ever did was to get us to America."

While they were talking, Willow was watching the clouds behind them. When Mitch had unloaded their canoe from his pickup and watched them glide out into the river, his last words were, "The forecast is for rain, but it's not supposed to come until afternoon." He was aware of the buildup of clouds to the southwest. "But be sure to get off the river if it does rain."

"I know, Mitch," she had said, "I know." Just because she'd spent a few years in New York didn't mean that she had forgotten how to survive on an Ozark stream.

She was remembering Mitch's worry as she scanned the sky. From the blackness of the approaching clouds and the lightning she could see streaking through them, she knew it was raining hard upriver.

"Maybe we better paddle some." She reached out in front to take a deep thrust with her paddle. The canoe's speed increased. Then she noticed the swell in the middle of the river that indicated that the water was rising. As they floated to a gravel bar she watched a mussel shell lying at the edge of the water half submerged. When she passed the bar and looked back, the shell was completely under water.

"What's the hurry?" Hugh said. He was enjoying the leisurely float and their togetherness. He sat on the front seat with his paddle across his lap. "Mitch won't be at the ford to pick us up until after lunch."

"The river's rising. And"—she pointed behind them—"look back there at the storm that's coming our way. On these little rivers and creeks water can go crazy in just minutes after a downpour upstream. Water runs off quickly in these hills. Not much soil to absorb it. Then all the little creeks and draws empty quickly into the river. That storm coming looks like a big one." She leaned over to take a more powerful stroke. Hugh began paddling on the opposite side.

With the rise in the river and their rapid paddling, the canoe glided almost soundlessly through the water, which was becoming increasingly browner. Low rumbles of thunder reached them.

"The storm's coming this way," Willow said. She was trying to remember where the best place would be to pull out. She was not worried, though to be on the safe side, she knew that they should get off the river before long. But she wanted to get as close as possible to the ford and the protection of the cabin. Picturing the bends, the gravel bars, and riffles in her mind, she believed they could easily reach the gravel bar where they ate lunch the first trip—the one just under the bluff from the cabin. That was about a river mile closer than the ford. They could beach the canoe on the bar, tie it to a big tree trunk, swim across the river, and climb the path to the cabin. There they could wait out the storm and afterward hike down the trail to meet Mitch, as scheduled, at the ford.

"Paddle hard." She had to speak louder as the wind

And Tyler, Too?

was whistling down the open eddy between the lines of trees on the banks. "We'll tie up at the cabin rather than going on down to the ford."

Hugh nodded. His powerful strokes from the front doubled their speed. "Yo ho, heave ho," he sang happily, keeping time with his paddle. He was thoroughly enjoying the ride, as if he were in an amusement park where there were thrills without any danger. He was unaware of Willow's growing alarm.

The storm behind them must have been a gully washer, because the water rose more rapidly than Willow anticipated. They entered the next riffle too rapidly. The vee of the current entering the narrow chute was a torrent of whitecaps. Twigs and leaves rushed along beside them as the current sucked them in. The normal lapping and easy falling of water through the narrowed passageway ahead had become an ominous roar from the extra load of water spilling through.

Willow leaned to the left to look around Hugh to see what was ahead. Although she was familiar with the turns of this riffle, she never assumed what would be ahead. The river constantly changed. Hugh held his paddle in the air in front of him, his left hand near the blade and his right hand gripping the tee at the top of the handle. He was poised ready to use it as a pole or a paddle, whichever was necessary to turn the craft and prevent it from striking boulders or trees.

"Duck!" he yelled as he bent forward in his seat. Big sycamore leaves brushed across his back as he slid under the overhanging tree. There was only a few inches of space between the white tree trunk and his T-shirt stretched across his back. Warned, Willow also leaned over. Neither had time to think about wiping from their heads the cobwebs and lint from the broad leaves as the water carried them swiftly on.

"Rock to the right!" Hugh yelled.

Willow compensated by back-paddling as hard as she could on the left.

"Tree down dead ahead."

Willow saw it at the same time. It lay half submerged almost across the narrow water path. Most of the water went under the trunk. The only way around it was a ninety-degree turn to the right almost to the edge of the water and then another sharp turn to the left. There was enough water that ran over the graveled shoreline to float the canoe if they could make both turns.

Several hard backstrokes on her right and Hugh's thrust against the fallen trunk with his paddle forced the bow of the canoe far enough to the right that they didn't crash head-on into the uprooted tree. But the left side of the canoe slammed against the trunk, knocking Willow to her knees. The left underside of the canoe scraped along the length of the log as the canoe leaned over to the right at a precarious angle. Hugh let go of his paddle as he grabbed the gunnels to keep from spilling out. The paddle rode the waves for a couple of seconds before being sucked under the tree with the main current. Kneeling, blinded briefly by the wall of water that washed in, Willow held to the crossbar and her paddle.

"Lead toward the log!" Willow managed to yell. Their combined weight prevented the canoe from overturning.

The momentum of the canoe carried it, bumping and scraping, along the tree log. At the end of the

And Tyler, Too?

trunk when it reached the shallow water, the canoe righted itself. Even though heavily laden with water, Willow made the left turn around the log. The bottom scraped on the gravel, the right side slammed against some rocks. As if it were a pole, Willow thrust her paddle into the loose gravel bottom and heaved up to keep the canoe from stopping. Free of the gravel and back in the swift current, the canoe shot out unharmed into the next eddy.

It started to sprinkle, though neither Willow nor Hugh noticed whether the water spraying their faces was rain or spray from the river. Willow had regained her seat and was paddling to the center of the river where it would be safer.

When it was safe to do so, Hugh turned around. "You okay?" he asked, though he really didn't need to. He could see she once again had control of the canoe. Her answer was to push forward to him the extra paddle lying on the bottom of the canoe under the crossbars. She waved away his suggestion to retrieve his lost paddle, which was caught on some brush behind them.

"That was some ride." The thrill of the ride and his admiration for her showed in his face.

"Piece of cake," she tried to say lightly, though she was still shaking from the near catastrophe. She knew how powerful was the force of the whole river spewing under that tree. If they had capsized there and been pulled under in that deep water ... She shuddered to think of the result. But no harm done, except a lost paddle. Mitch would probably find it later.

Though she rarely wore life vests on this normally mild river where they could wade in most places, after their narrow escape, she thought it prudent to put them on now. Reaching under her seat she pulled out two red adult vests—one which she strapped onto herself and the other which she tossed to Hugh.

In the open water with no immediate emergency ahead, Willow took time to review their moves in the riffle. She smiled in satisfaction. Not bad. When she thought of Hugh's quick thinking, she knew they made a good team. She and Mitch could not have done better. Well, maybe. Mitch probably wouldn't have lost his paddle, but no big deal.

But they were still on the river, which within minutes had advanced to white-water difficulty. The last riffle was just an example of what might be ahead. But warned and being careful, they should be fine. Nothing much to worry about the rest of the way. "The cabin is in the next eddy, about a mile on down. Want to try for it?" she asked.

"Sure."

"Just one more riffle."

"Riffle? That sounds so innocuous. Rapids is more like it."

They both paddled as in a race—which in truth they were, in a race with the storm. "When we reach the next riffle, let's slow down before we enter to give us a chance to see what's ahead." She saw the back of his head nod vigorously. "If it looks bad, we'll get out." Again he nodded agreement.

The thunder behind them was louder, but still a distance away. Lightning continued to flick from the black clouds that seemed closer every time Willow looked back. They both now recognized the water hitting their faces as rain. It was colder than the river

And Tyler, Too? 133

water, and though the air temperature was in the upper 80s, the rain and wind made her shiver from the contrast.

This is not a good idea, Willow kept telling herself. *Get off the river.* But she didn't stop paddling. Though they were both working as hard as before, the canoe didn't skim over the surface as fast because its extra load of water made it float deeper. There was no time to bail it out, or do what she and Mitch usually did when they used to ship water—take it to shore and dump out the water. As these possibilities coursed through her head, she heeded only her goal, which had became a command. *Get to the gravel bar by the cabin. The gravel bar by the cabin.* Its pulling power was stronger than her reasoning and good sense. *The cabin.*

As if proving her decision was correct, the last riffle, instead of being treacherous, was almost nonexistent. The high water level allowed them to float right over rocks that normally detoured the current up against the bluff. The two eddies almost blended into one.

"Yee-e-e hi-eye-eye-eye!" Hugh called, waving his wet straw hat in the air as they turned the easy bend from the riffle onto the open waters of the Dawson Eddy. About three-fourths down the eddy across from their picnic spot, he spotted the white bark of the sycamore tree and the rope hanging down from its branch. But his elation stopped when he noticed that the end of the rope was in the water. Before it was a good two feet above it. Then he shot a worried look at Willow when he couldn't see the gravel bar. It was completely covered with rushing water. Behind the row of willows on the bar was a steep mudbank. On their right was the bluff to the cabin. No place to put in on either side, and the current was carrying them on to the next riffle that was roaring louder than any so far. Beyond the rope swing where the riverbed narrowed, water was swirling with foaming whitecaps.

"Back-paddle," Willow called. They would float right by the spot and be sucked into the rough water unless she found a place to pull in. She had to make a quick decision. The water was rising so rapidly that Hugh noticed it. The thunder and lightning were right behind them. They had to get off the river. Now!

Ahead, just beyond the sycamore, she saw some willows spaced along the edge under the bluff. "Over to the right to those willows!" she shouted. The wind was stronger and rain was beating down on them in gusts. For answer, Hugh brought the bow around to point it from the center of the river right into the bluff and the trees. Together they forced the canoe across the strong current. Just as they approached the first tree head-on, Willow forced the stern around to the right, straightening the canoe to go parallel to the bluff under the overhanging limbs. When headed in the direction she wanted, she back-paddled to almost stop their movement.

"I got the canoe!" she shouted. "You grab on to one of those trees."

Hugh didn't take time to answer. Knowing what she had in mind, he seized the rope tied to the bow of the canoe with one hand. With the other he reached up, and holding securely to a sturdy-looking branch, wound the rope quickly around it. At the same time Willow grabbed a limb above her. Her branch was smaller and bent with the weight. But it slowed them

And Tyler, Too?

enough for Hugh to secure his rope. The sudden jerk when Hugh's rope took hold and abruptly stopped the canoe caused Willow's grip to slip. With neither Willow nor Hugh in control, the canoe eased away from the bluff enough to catch the current. The back end swung out into the river to the left. Willow's weight, as she leaned to the right to hold on to the branch, tipped the canoe enough that more water poured in.

Willow's branch broke. She went over the side and completely disappeared in the rushing water, though the life vest pulled her right up. When she surfaced, she found herself being carried downstream. As she shook the water from her eyes, she saw that the canoe had completely reversed directions. Its left side was pinned against the row of willow trees. Its bow, still securely tied to the branch, was now pointed upstream. Hugh was scrambling from it onto the rocky ledge along the bluff. He managed to fight his way through the limber tree branches along the precarious bluff rocks to keep up with Willow.

Taking advantage of the river's current rather than fighting it, she swam for a boulder that jutted out from the bluff at the downstream end of the line of trees. She heard a sharp crack followed by a loud clap of thunder. Too close. It was imperative she get out of the water. With all the strength she could muster and some extra that she didn't know she had, she fought the current and reached the rock. It was smooth on that side and slippery with wet moss. Her hand slipped off. The swirl of the current around the rock sucked her into it and propelled her with it to the backside of the boulder. There she was carried under another willow tree. When she grabbed the long hanging branch of this tree, it held, though it bent down into the water with her weight and the tug of the current against her.

"Hang on!" Hugh shouted. He climbed over the boulder and into the lower branches of the tree as far out as the limbs could hold his weight.

Willow was still floating in water too deep for her to touch bottom, but her movement downstream was checked. She was hanging on to the end of the limber limb that was stretched out into the river as far as it could go.

"Hang on!" Hugh yelled again. The rain swept across the river in powerful gusts. The last clap of thunder seemed just up the eddy. Sky, rain, and river all mingled together into one gray wetness. "The limb is strong. It won't break."

In spite of her danger Willow realized that it was a willow tree that could save her life. Even the Indians couldn't have come up with a better name for her. Somehow the thought that it was a willow tree and not a sycamore or maple calmed her and allowed her to think clearly. Hugh was helpless to rescue her. If he climbed out on the limb it would surely break. He couldn't reach her from the bluff. The current was too strong for him to swim in after her. It would sweep him away. It was up to her and her willow tree.

Carefully releasing her left hand, but holding tight with her right hand, she forced her left hand up the limb above the other hand. *Good.* Then she did the same thing with her right hand. She and Mitch used to have contests to see which one of them could shinny up a rope the fastest. She often won. This was the same thing, only she wasn't in quite the same physical condition, and the current was holding her, sucking

And Tyler, Too?

her down. The rain in her eyes almost blinded her. And the thunder! She heard another sharp electric crack where lightning struck something not too far away, and then a deafening clap of thunder that continued in a decreasing rumble that rolled over her.

Mustn't think about that. Got to beat Mitch. She put one hand over the other, pulling herself closer and closer to the tree trunk where Hugh was perched with one hand outstretched to seize her the second she got close enough. *Got to beat Mitch.*

She wasn't delirious. She had been thinking so much about Mitch, and this escapade with Hugh was so much like those she and Mitch used to get into, that she reverted a moment to her girlhood. *Stupid! I'm not a child anymore, and that is Hugh there.* She looked up. Under his hat's broad brim dripping with water, she saw his black eyes frantic with worry.

"Don't worry, Hugh," she said aloud, "I got it made."

Her next grab up the limb met Hugh's hand. She was whooshed out of the river and into his arms just as another peal of thunder roared. As he held her, he was facing downstream, she upstream. "Look!" she cried, pointing up the river. There was a wall of water at least three feet high rolling toward them. They jumped on top of the boulder and started scaling the cliff to a narrow ledge. The muddy, swollen river, twice its normal size and suddenly three feet higher, roared beneath them, completely covering the boulder they just left. The willow tree that saved Willow bowed as the water covered it. Only the top branches bending downstream with the current showed where it was.

"Can't stay here!" Willow shouted above the cacophony of thunder, wind, and a river gone mad. "There's a way to the cabin from here. Mitch and I . . ." She didn't finish. No need to explain the secret paths she and Mitch knew. They needed to get out of the storm as quickly as possible. The wind that had been steadily blowing from the southwest was beginning to buffet them from all directions. She feared it was a tornado, though a quick look to the southwest did not show a funnel. Probably couldn't see it now with the storm upon them.

The cabin was their salvation. It had stood since 1861 through woods fires, storms, and war. They'd find shelter there.

Holding tight to Hugh's hand as if she would lose him to the storm if she let go, she skirted the bluff. Each one supported the other as they found foot- and hand-holds. She led the way into a crevice, and avoiding the water that gushed down it, they climbed up a half-eroded path. They had to duck under trees and logs and climb over fallen debris and rocks long ago washed down from the ridge. In places they had to let go of each other's hands to get around some obstacle, but once on the way again Willow clutched Hugh's hand.

When they reached the top of the bluff, they ran through the woods to the unused trail leading from the cabin to the old ford. From there it was a quick sprint to the cabin.

They pushed open the heavy door and then closed it securely behind them. The battle outside of all nature gone mad could not penetrate the log walls. They clung to each other. Water streamed from their hair and clothes onto puddles on the puncheon floor. It formed into tiny rivulets and disappeared between the cracks. The wind howled around the corners and stirred up some old ashes left in the fireplace, but didn't touch them. The ear-splitting booms of thunder were softened by the thick log walls. In the semidarkness of the cabin, with its boarded windows, the frightening and eerie light from the almost constant flashes of lightning had little effect. On three sides, except for the rocky glade in front, tall ancient oaks, hickories, and walnuts protected the cabin as they had been doing for decades.

Willow and Hugh were safe.

Chapter Twelve

Neither Willow nor Hugh said anything. Breathless, they stumbled to a bench to sit down. Hugh's arm circled Willow as she rested her head on his chest. Even over the noise outside, she could hear his heart beating rapidly. After they sat there for a few minutes it resumed its normal rate.

In the cocoon of the cabin with its covered windows, they could not see outside. Between the claps and roar of the thunder they heard trees snapping and cracking. Once there was a big thud, as of one falling over very near. The wind buffeted the log house from all sides, but the walls held strong. The roof held. Only the loose boards tacked carelessly over the windows rattled. One flopped and banged for a few minutes and then flew off. They watched it soar in the air like a piece of paper until it disappeared from their line of vision.

Water blew in through the gap in the window, but did not reach them. Outside they could see the rain blown almost horizontal from the force of the wind. Leaves and other debris swirled around the cabin, flying in every direction. Several oak leaves and twigs

And Tyler, Too?

were sucked through the window and landed on the floor beside them.

Gradually the noise moved away from them as the center of the storm moved on. The wind slackened. The rain slowed and gradually stopped altogether. Only then did the two stand up and, still holding tight to each other, venture to the window.

Sheets of water were still pouring over the rocky glade and spilling down the bluff to the river. The lone oak that shaded the rock slab was down, its sagging crown hanging over the bluff. They saw a couple of uprooted cedar trees near the path down to the river, but the large trees around them stood, their wet leaves drooping, the ground under them strewn with branches and limbs. In the distant northeast they heard the fading rumbles of the storm as it wore itself out.

In contrast to the cacophony earlier, the world was silent. Hugh pulled back the heavy door. They stepped outside. The air was fresh, but still warm against their soaked clothing. The wind was now a balmy summer breeze, tugging at their shirttails. A red squirrel scampered through the tall trees and jumped onto the cabin roof. He watched Hugh and Willow a few seconds before silently leaping to an oak branch. They watched him vault from tree to tree until they lost sight of him.

But the world wasn't quiet, just hushed. A sad-sounding bobwhite call came from behind the cabin. He called twice before there was an answering call to their left. Insect noises began their soft background humming. Below the bluff they could hear the muted roar of the river. And, incredibly, they heard the traffic on the highway five miles away.

Their shoes squished as they walked over the rock glade to the top of the bluff to look at the river. Hugh swung out his arm to indicate the view below and shook his head in wonder at the much-changed scene. The river water was over the bottom field. The soybeans were covered, but the corn tops farthest from the river stood up in green rows from their watery bed. In the spaces between the lines of trees bordering the river, they could see the turbulent, brown water surging madly on.

As Hugh stared in wonder, all he could think of to say was, "And you said nothing exciting ever happens here."

His light tone broke the spell. "I lied," she said. They both laughed in relief that the storm was over and they were both unhurt. "Everything seems to be all right."

Hugh looked at her in disbelief. "All right? Tippy, my love, we've lost Mitch's canoe and paddles, not to mention the lunch. The crops are ruined, Mitch is probably frantic about us, and..." He looked around at the tangle of limbs all over the yard. "... and the road is about to wash out around that rock and we've got a mess to clean up."

Willow laughed again at his calling her Tippy, because once again she'd earned the name. Though she pretended not to hear him, she didn't miss his adding, "my love."

"No, Hugh, it's not so bad. First, the canoe will ride out the flood. We used to keep our boats tied to the river all the time. Saves hauling them, but since we moved to town, we don't anymore. Mitch can get it and probably find the paddles and lunch cooler.

And Tyler, Too?

They'll get hung up on some limbs or rocks. Though I'll admit the sandwiches will be rather soggy, the sodas will be okay.''

She pointed to the field. ''The water will go down quickly. By morning it will probably be back in its banks. It won't do much damage to the crops. Won't do the soybeans any good, but they'll survive. It won't hurt the corn at all, just give it a good drink. And the hay field. It's already harvested. The silt the river leaves will enrich the ground and maybe with the extra moisture, we'll get another cutting from it in the fall.''

She walked back toward the cabin. ''No problem to clean up the tree branches. If you still want to rough it after this, there's your firewood. And this rock here.'' She stepped on to the big flat rock they used to spread out their lunches. ''All it needs is some of that gravel that you told Dad you'd haul up for him.''

Hugh looked at her in amazement. ''Incredible!''

Willow looked at the slab more closely. ''Say, it's washed out more than I've ever seen it.'' They stepped on it and it wobbled noticeably.

''I better get at that right away,'' Hugh said. ''That's one of the jobs I'll do for my rent here.''

Willow looked at the cabin as if she had never seen it before. ''I take back what I said about your staying here in Grandma Edna's house. I do know why you want to.''

Hugh ran his hand over her hair which was almost dry. Then he ran his fingers down to her chin. Lifting it up to make her look at him he said, ''You sensed it, didn't you?''

Willow knew what he meant. ''Yes.''

''Inside there's a peace . . . no, more like a comfort

or . . . security—yes, that's it. Security. I've felt it every time I've been here."

Willow nodded. "I never thought about it. I've known this place all my life, so it has always had a comfortable feeling for me. I always had a sense of ownership, or a tie back to something very important. Even Dad senses that. It's why he has indulged Mom whenever she wanted to do anything here, though he makes noises about how ridiculous the legend is and all. He knows there's more here than that."

"But you felt it even more when we came in here out of the storm. I could tell. You were tight as a drum, but when we got inside, you relaxed."

"Yes, I did. I feel absolutely safe here. Like nothing can harm me." She looked around at the unscathed cabin. Then she saw an uprooted cedar tree behind the cabin that fell away from the building. "And I was right."

They marveled that they both sensed the same magical force. Willow sat down on the rock slab. With the recent erosion on the cabin side of the slab, it made a not-too-uncomfortable seat about a foot from the ground.

"Is this the feeling that you're trying to capture in your sketches?" Willow asked.

"Yes. It's all interwoven with this land and its moods and the people who settled it and stayed here. Like your parents. Like Mitch."

"But not like me?"

"Yes, like you, too. And about the people who needed something more. Obviously lots of people who came here didn't stay. I want to show that, too, and what made them leave."

"Money," Willow said, smiling.

"That and more. Until today, I'd have portrayed it as all beautiful weather with prospering plants and animals. Kind of a modern Eden."

"It's far from that."

"Don't I know. We just experienced one of its serpents."

"A very long one, if you're thinking about the river. But it'll be a pussycat again in a few days."

Without realizing the time, they wandered around the grounds talking and inspecting the damage to the trees. Willow didn't think about how late it was getting until she felt hunger pangs and noticed how low in the western sky was the sun that was just peeking out from behind the clouds.

"Mitch must be worried sick," she said suddenly. "He has no idea where we are or if we got off the river."

"Maybe we should go to the farmhouse and telephone."

Just when they started hiking down the trail, they heard a vehicle approaching. Mitch's truck skidded to a stop in front of them. He jumped out the door and ran to them. Both worry and anger showed on his face. He grabbed Willow in a hug and patted Hugh's shoulder as if to prove he was real.

"Willow! Hugh! You okay? I can see you are. Been here all the time? Why didn't you call? I've been sick with worry. Uncle Jerry's hitting all the access points on the other side of the river. Thought you were drowned." He said all this in one rush of words. Then without waiting for them to reply, he crawled back in his cab to his cellular phone. "They're at the Dawson cabin," he said when Jerry answered on the first ring. "They're all right. Yeah, I'm sure. They are fine. Yeah, everything here seems fine. No major damage I can see. Yeah, I'll bring them straight home. Right. See you in half an hour."

He hung up his receiver, slid over to open the passenger door, and said, "Get in. I've got orders to take you home."

"Yes, sir," Willow said and laughed.

"I see you found our cooler," Hugh said. He peered in the window of the pickup shell. Before getting in beside Willow, he opened the back hatch to inspect the cooler. It was still closed. He pulled out three sodas and, closing the hatch, came to the cab. He gave Willow and Mitch each a cold can. "Shouldn't we unload my stuff while we're here?"

"Later. I better get you home or Uncle Jerry will have a coronary." Mitch turned around and bumped down the trail, driving very slowly because of the deep gullies washed out around the rocks in the road by the recent storm.

"Where'd you find the cooler?" Willow asked, popping the cap of the soda. "And how did you know we were here?"

"Well, when the storm hit," Mitch said, taking a long swig at his drink, "I didn't think much about it. I figured you'd pull off and then hike to the nearest phone and call me. But then I got to thinking about when you left and how much time you would have had on the river before the storm hit you. I figured that you would try to outrun the storm. Was I right?"

Willow nodded.

"So I waited out the storm and drove to the ford.

You weren't there. So I figured you would have pulled off earlier. Then I saw the cooler snagged against a tree. The cooler was easy to get. When I opened it, I saw that you hadn't eaten anything. I figured you'd swamped, for if you'd just pulled off the river, you'd have taken the cooler, or at least put it out of reach of the water. Uncle Jerry called me, worried as heck. He said he'd go to all the usual places on the west side of the river to see if you were there, while I checked on this side. We kept each other informed. We thought that something must have happened or you would have called.

"I figured that since the cooler made it this far, that you and the canoe weren't too far upriver. Uncle Jerry drove as close as he could get to the gravel bar by the swimming hole. He saw the canoe tied to a willow and upside down. Now that could be good news. You guys got out, tied it up, and were up at the cabin.... Or you tied it up and before you got out, the canoe swamped and you were swept down the river. Or drowned right there.

"So I cut up here to see. I checked again with the folks at the farmhouse. They hadn't seen you, so I thought for sure that you were goners. You'd have surely gone there to call." He stopped in his recital and faced Willow. "Why on earth didn't you?" He was as angry as he ever got. "You've had plenty of time to let us know. You're not in New York where no one gives a hoot about you. Where you can be killed on the street and no one will stop to help. You're here, home with us. We're all connected whether you like it or not. You can't go around so independent, with no consideration of us."

"I'm sorry, Mitch. I didn't think," Willow said. She couldn't remember Mitch ever talking to her like this before. All she could do was repeat, "I'm sorry." She set her empty can in Mitch's recycling sack for aluminum cans.

"We almost did drown," Hugh said, trying to explain. "And while we hung on to the edge of the bluff, we went through the worst storm I ever saw. When we reached the cabin, all we could think of was..."

"I know, Tyler," Mitch said. He wasn't angry anymore. "It must have been awful out in that. I didn't know how bad the storm was here until I got back. It wasn't bad at all in town. Just a hard shower for a few minutes. But from the looks of the river at the ford and all the tree damage, I figured it must have been a twister here."

"I think it was," Willow said. "But Mitch, nothing fazed the cabin. It was safe inside."

"Good thing we put on the new roof, huh?" His pleasant nature returned.

"Just in time," Hugh said.

"Well," Mitch said, "no harm done, and all that. Phew!" He let out a big breath and turned his smiling face to them as he paused for Hugh to open the gate at the farm. "All's well that ends well."

Mitch laughed when he caught the exchange of glances between Willow and Hugh. "I tell you what let's do, guys. Willow doesn't leave until Sunday. This is Friday. What say we all come back to the cabin tomorrow for a farewell picnic? All of us? Then we can move Tyler in, since I wouldn't let him today. And retrieve the canoe."

"Sounds good to me," Hugh said.

And Tyler, Too?

Mitch looked from him to Willow. Hugh was holding her hand, or was it the other way around? He noticed how close they were sitting together and how often they looked at each other.

"Mission almost accomplished," Mitch said very softly.

"What did you say?" Willow asked.

"Oh, nothing. Just glad that you are all right." He winked at Hugh.

"I saw that, and I heard what you said, Mitchy-boy." Willow used the pet name that she hadn't used since grade-school days. "You think you're pretty clever, don't you?"

"Matter of fact, I do, Willow-Wallow."

Willow slapped him playfully on his arm.

Mitch turned into the graveled farm road and on to the highway. The events of the day were taking their toll on all of them. No one said anything as they neared the edge of town.

Willow was reviewing in her mind her decision on the river to keep paddling rather than taking out when it started to rain. It was a risky move, but as it turned out, she succeeded in what she wanted to do. They did get to the Dawson Eddy and to the cabin as she planned. Just some extra excitement thrown in for spice.

Squeezed between her cousin and Hugh in Mitch's small pickup cab, she continued her comparison of the two. Mitch still maintained a sort of proprietary air toward her of the older cousin. Older by only three months, but he had played that for all he could when they were kids. Hugh, on the other hand, never bossed her or pointed out any mistakes or flaws. Without consciously planning it, she pressed his hand. He squeezed back.

Then the image of the cabin came to her with its sense of security. She pictured again the scene she and Hugh saw when they stepped out of the door when the storm was over.

She jerked up, startling both men.

"What's the matter?" Mitch asked. He looked at her rapt expression as she stared out the windshield. "See a ghost down the road or something?"

"No, not a ghost. Well, maybe yes. I guess it is a ghost. Mitch, Hugh"—she turned to each of them—"I know where Grandpa Ben's payroll is."

"Yeah, yeah," Mitch said. "And I know where the Loch Ness monster lives."

"No, Mitch, this time I really do."

Hugh showed no surprise, as if he knew all along that she would find it. Her present affirmation only proved he was right. "I think she really does know, Mitch," he said.

"You're both crazy. You've swallowed too much river water."

"I'll show you tomorrow. But you and Charley and Gene have to bring some stuff."

"What stuff?"

"Charley will need to bring his small wrecker. I'll make a list for the rest." She grabbed a pad and pencil Mitch had tucked under a clip on his sun visor. Willow wrote down several items and after showing the sheet to Hugh, handed it to Mitch.

He read the list. His only comment was, "Humph!"

"But you'll get them?"

"Fool's notion." He looked at her eager face and

And Tyler, Too?

raised eyebrows. He could never refuse her when she was determined. "Okay. I'll ask Charley to come in his small wrecker, and I'll get the rest. Satisfied?"

"Yes, Mitch. You're the best. You'll be glad. I know I'm right."

"Your mother thought she was right when she made Uncle Jerry climb all over Fall-in-Bluff."

"But since then we've found Grandma Edna's note."

Chapter Thirteen

"Okay, Willow," Mitch said the next day when the whole family was at the cabin, "now what's this all about?"

"Yeah," Charley said, scratching his thinning black hair. "I've got the small wrecker you wanted. I can't imagine why."

"She's gonna find Grandpa Ben's money, Daddy," Cory said. He and Dawn had been pestering Willow to tell them more ever since they got there. "Where is it, Aunt Willow?"

"You'll see," was all Willow would say.

Charley shrugged his shoulders at Mitch. "Well, since it's Willow's last day home, I guess we can humor her." He inspected the cabin roof. "Good job, guys."

"I helped, Daddy," Cory said.

"Me, too, Uncle Charley," Dawn said. "And Barney, too." She hugged the collie.

"Yeah, I heard." Charley stepped into the cabin and took in the dusty interior. "We better get to work and clean up this place a bit if Tyler's going to bunk here."

Maggie was already carrying in brooms and mops.

And Tyler, Too? 153

Mitch and Amy were carrying in Hugh's things left in his pickup shell from yesterday.

"But the gold, Aunt Willow." Cory was hanging on to her arm. The suspense was too much for him. How could adults just go calmly about cleaning house and unpacking when Willow was about to give them the solution to a century-old mystery?

Willow was also impatient. Not one of her family, except the children, was taking her seriously. Sure, they brought the stuff she asked—she made certain of that—but they were obviously doing it just to humor her, treating her as if she were Cory or Dawn. Being the youngest in her family, she was used to their indulgent behavior toward her. In spite of her success in the fashion field, to them she was still the little sister. Usually it was easier to play along with them on her infrequent visits home, but this time was different. She was dead serious.

As she watched her parents and sisters-in-law clean out the cabin and her brothers and Mitch making quick work of unloading her auction purchases and Hugh's things, she also noticed Hugh. He was standing out of their way beside Mitch's pickup. Like Willow and the children, he seemed impatient with the others. Not once since she announced yesterday that she knew where the payroll was did he show disbelief. Confident she knew what she was doing, he was ready to do whatever she asked. Nor did he pester her to tell him how she figured out the payroll hiding place. When Willow's eyes met his, he spread out his hands to indicate his awareness of how futile it was to change the others. "Might as well let them finish first," he suggested.

"Actually, it's a good idea," she said. "When we do find the money, they'll be too excited to do anything else. We might as well get the chores done."

"Yes," was all Hugh said. He didn't correct her to say, "*If* we find the money." Nor did he give that maddening, let's-humor-baby-sister smirk Charley and Gene gave when she talked about it.

The men unloaded quickly. Then with Mitch in the lead they hiked down the bluff path to look at the river and to see about the canoe.

"Might as well join them," Willow said, taking Hugh's hand and following them.

The river was still high, but, as Willow had predicted, it was back within its banks. The canoe was still tied to the willow tree, half hanging and half submerged. Only the part in front of the seat was above water. Mitch, Charley, and Gene scrambled over the rocks to the willow tree. With ropes and a grappling hook they pulled it onto the narrow ledge under the bluff and dumped out the water. They debated what to do with it. Since the paddles were gone and they hadn't thought to bring extra ones, they couldn't take it across the river or float downstream to the takeout place at the old ford.

"Why not just leave it here?" Willow said. "It'll be okay."

"No," Mitch said. "I'll need it before I get back to the river. Besides, I've got the manpower to move it now."

"We can take it up the bluff," Charley suggested.

"Are you crazy?" Willow said, and threw up her hands. She knew that was what they would do.

Charley and Gene were already tying long ropes to

the crossbars of the canoe. Mitch replaced the frayed rope already on the front with a stronger one. The three men eased the canoe back in the river and, guiding it with the ropes as they crawled along the shore, pulled the floating canoe upstream to the path. From there, as long as they were in the bottom field, it was easy with a man on either side to portage the canoe. But the going became difficult when they came to the narrow, steep path up the bluff.

"Willow, you and Tyler bring up the rear. Push or lift it if needed," Mitch said. "Charley, Gene, and I will pull it up."

"You're crazy," Willow said again.

"No more than you were to get it here in the first place," Gene said.

Willow made a face at him. He had a point. "Why not leave it here in the field and when the ground dries out, come after it in your pickup?" Mitch didn't answer.

With all of them pulling, pushing, and lifting, it wasn't as difficult as Willow thought to get the light canoe up the bluff. The children and Jerry were on top cheering them on. Barney ran back and forth down the path and back to the children, wanting to be in both places at once. When they reached the top, Mitch and Charley easily lifted the canoe onto the racks on Mitch's truck.

That chore taken care of, Willow and Hugh entered the cabin. It looked like a different place. When they came in out of the storm it offered security. Now it had charm. *Cozy* might be a word to describe its appearance. The women had scrubbed it. Jerry had removed the boards over the two front windows and tacked clear plastic to let in light. The surviving furniture—table, bench, and other odds and ends—were cleaned and arranged invitingly with the rocker, cupboard, and stool Willow had bought at the sale. And, though Hugh had forbidden it, Maggie had brought a few essentials she didn't think he would think of, such as a water bucket, dipper, and slop bucket.

"Didn't think you'd know to get them," Maggie apologized when Hugh frowned at her, "never having lived without running water."

"But I have," Hugh said. He tilted his head and smiled. "Up until I was nine."

"Score one for Hugh," Willow said, laughing at her mother's dismayed face.

Hugh's bags and the camping equipment borrowed from Mitch were piled in the corner. On the old maple table, splotched with water spots and marred with years of use and neglect, was spread out a dinner. Each family had brought dishes of food, but, as usual, Maggie outdid them all with her fried chicken, new potatoes and baby onions, fresh garden salad, wheat rolls, and homemade blackberry cobbler, the children's favorite.

"When I'm with my family," Willow whispered to Hugh when he asked her when they would let her explain about the payroll, "my time's not my own. Not even my life. So, I might as well go along with them and let them play out their hand."

Now that the cabin was cleaned and presentable, they didn't eat outside on the rock slab. Besides, it was too hot on the rock now that the oak that used to shade it was down. People filed by to fill their paper plates. Except for Willow, the other women sat at the table on the

And Tyler, Too?

bench. "First time in two generations anyone has eaten from this table," Maggie said proudly. The men went outside to sit in the lawn chairs Maggie had brought. Though first through the line, the children waited to see where Willow and Hugh would go so they could sit by them. Willow chose the fallen oak log.

"Where's the gold?" Cory asked. Even if everyone else had forgotten, he hadn't.

Willow gave a sigh of exasperation and said, "Maybe after dinner the rest will let me tell them. Be patient just a bit longer."

"You can tell *us*," Dawn said. Her mouth was smeared with ketchup and her blouse and shorts grubby from wiping her greasy hands on them. She was feeding Barney half of the food on her plate. "Me and Barney and Cory and Hugh. We believe you."

"And I appreciate that, pumpkin, but I'll wait. I want everybody to hear it all at the same time."

After the meal, Maggie spread a white cloth over the leftover food to keep the flies off. She didn't put the food away in case someone might want more. The children gathered up the paper plates and cups into a plastic garbage bag. When all the chores were done, and before Jerry or one of her brothers could suggest clearing the branches out of the yard or hiking down to the bottom to look at the crops now that the water had receded, Willow decided this was the time. Everyone was lounging in the shade in front of the cabin, content from their meal and being with one another.

Willow stood up ready to begin, though nobody paid any attention to her. She looked at Hugh. He nodded encouragement and grinned. "Wow 'em," he said.

"You know, don't you?"

He nodded. "I have a pretty good idea."

Mitch poked Hugh. He was sitting between Hugh and Amy. "No private tête-à-têtes here, Tyler my man. Here Willow's business is everyone's business."

"Yes, Willow," Amy said, sending her a look that said she understood, but she was having too much fun to back off. "This is your last day. You're leaving and Tyler's staying. C'mon, give. What's with you two?"

Though the subject was not what she wanted, this was the opening Willow needed. Mitch and Amy's remarks made her the center of attention. This subject was one they were interested in, for they were all in league with pairing her up with Hugh. She had the floor.

"Okay, you guys. Hugh and I have been business associates in New York for some time. Now, thanks to all of you"—Willow paused while they laughed and looked at one another with satisfaction—"now after this vacation together, we've become friends." She ignored the affected groans from Charley and Mitch's I-know-better expression. "But Hugh and I aren't what I want to talk to you about, and you know it." Quickly then, before someone said something to take the floor from her or change the subject, she repeated what she had told them earlier. "I know where Ben Dawson hid the Union payroll in 1862."

Although she held up her hand to forestall the comments she expected, nobody said a word. She stood before them in rolled-up denim shorts and a long blue T-shirt the color of her eyes that lacked only three inches from coming to the folded hems of her shorts. Her hair was tousled, and on her feet she wore only her old and worn sneakers. But her manner and stance was that of an executive of Mansfield & Logan, Inc. For the first time her family recognized her commanding presence. They listened.

The silence was so unusual that Willow paused for a second before continuing. "All these years we've been looking in the wrong places. Even when Dawn found Grandma Edna's packet of Ben's letters and her note, we still didn't understand. We were getting closer. At least we knew that the legend was true. But yesterday Hugh and I stepped out of that cabin after the storm was over. I stood in the doorway and looked over this glade and over the bluff to see what damage there was. I saw this oak tree blown over. Then I remembered what Grandpa Ben said. He did tell his wife where he hid the money, and I knew what his words meant."

She stopped, expecting some comment. Silence. "Go on," Hugh urged.

"Okay, but before I do, I think there's something else we better decide on first." Cory and Dawn groaned at another delay just when she was going to tell them. "Just a little bit more, kids, but I think this is very important." To the group she said, "Hugh said something to me the other day that got me to thinking. He asked me what if we find the money? What then? I think we should all agree on what we'll do with it when we find it."

"*If* we find it," Jerry said.

"Right, Dad, if we find it. What will we do with it?"

No one said anything. The possibility was so unlikely that they hadn't considered it.

When she got no answer, Willow said, "I've been thinking about it and I think the first thing would be to see about the legality of it. Would it be ours? Maybe it still belongs to the army."

"Good point," Gene said. "I could check on that."

"Would you, Gene?" Willow continued. "Now let's assume that it is ours. Who does 'ours' mean? This land belongs to Mom and Dad. Is it theirs? Or should it be shared equally among all of Ben's and Edna's descendants? What do you think?"

"As far as I'm concerned," Jerry said, "it's Maggie's decision. This portion of our farm was her inheritance."

Maggie looked at Mitch, the only son of her sister, dead years ago. Without hesitation she said, "It belongs to all descendants equally."

Willow made a quick eye-contact check with Mitch, Amy, her brothers, and their wives. All agreed. "Okay, if the government has no claims on the money, it will be shared equally by all descendants. Since we here are the only descendants, and, counting the kids, that makes seven of us, what will we do with it?"

There was a long pause. No one had any suggestions.

Cory then said, "Put it in our corporation. We already own shares in it."

"Only we don't have any real money, just play money," Dawn said.

The adults exchanged glances. "The kids have a good idea," Gene said. He looked proudly at his daughter. His face broke into a grin, showing a dimple

And Tyler, Too? 161

just like Dawn's. "Our make-believe corporation could become a real one."

"And we could really restore this cabin," Mitch said.

"And if any of us have more children," Charley said, looking at Mitch and then at Willow, who ignored his implication, "they could automatically be part of it."

"And my kids and Cory's?" Dawn asked.

"Sure," Maggie said. "Keeps the heritage alive."

When there was a pause, Willow asked, "Any other suggestions?"

Maggie said, "Depending on how much the gold is worth, there may be enough to set up some sort of educational trust or foundation in addition to maintaining the cabin. Ben gave his life for his family. We should use it to improve the lives of his descendants. I can't think of a better way than through education."

"Excellent idea," Charley said.

"The details of the corporation and its purposes could be decided later," Gene said. "We must remember that all this is theoretical."

"Finding any money is theoretical," Mitch said, "but the cabin is real. We've already expended time, muscle, and some money on it. Whether we find the payroll or not, I say we incorporate anyway. Each of us can contribute something—time, household equipment and furniture, or their own money."

Cory said, "That's what we're already doing."

"Right, Cory," Willow said, "only Mitch's saying let's make it permanent and legal, not just make-believe." She looked at each in turn. Her brothers nodded. Maggie smiled broadly. She was all for it.

"Okay," Willow said. "Let's take a vote on how many are in favor of forming a family corporation to restore and preserve this cabin and maybe have some other objectives to promote the family heritage..." She paused to emphasize the next part. "...whether we find any money or not."

"Do in-laws get to vote?" Amy asked.

Jerry said, "I don't feel that I should."

"Me either," Charley's wife said.

"Okay with you, Amy?" Willow asked.

"Sure, I just wanted to know whether to vote."

"Is Barney an in-law?" Dawn wanted to know. The collie was lying quietly beside her.

"Stupid, 'course not," Cory said. "He's a dog. He can't vote."

"He can raise his paw, see?" Dawn held up his front leg. Cory wrinkled up his freckled nose at her.

Ignoring the children, Willow asked, "All in favor?"

Seven hands went up. "That's unanimous."

Dawn jerked on Willow's shirttail. "What does unan...mus mean?"

"It means that we all agree."

"Good." Dawn's smile spread over her face, showing a newly missing front tooth. "We are unanmus."

"Yes, it is good, Dawn. Sometimes families have trouble over money. That's why I wanted to get this decided now."

Charley turned to Gene. "Our little sister's gotten pretty smart. Now if she'll just be smart enough to..." He gave a knowing look at Hugh.

"Charley Hill!" Willow started to fall into his trap, acting like she used to when her big brothers teased

And Tyler, Too?

her. But she cut herself short. Now that she had the family's complete attention, she was anxious to get to her discovery.

"All right. We know what we'll do with the money when—okay, Dad—*if* we find it. Now back to what I have figured out. Before we got to what to do with the money, I was talking about what Ben Dawson said in Edna's note. Remember when we talked about this a few days ago we decided that Ben didn't have very much time to hide the payroll after he got home from the store? We estimated that he took his unit back to the store to 'lay a false trail,' as the story goes. We pretty well agreed then that the money was near the cabin."

Jerry, Maggie, and Mitch nodded.

"Now," Willow said, "let me read again Grandma Edna's note—the part that's important."

She pulled out of her pocket a crumpled sheet where she had copied the note. She read:

Just afore Ben and his soldiers left, he said some strange words to me. I didn't give it no mind at the time, but since then I've been studying on them, and I've about decided that they was not about us so much as about the payroll that he was carrying.

She stopped reading. "See, she believed that his words were clues to the location of the payroll. I do, too. Notice what she says next:"

He didn't say nothing to me about what he was doing that morning afore he left in such a hurry, but I thought then and still do now that he did something with the payroll.

"In other words he hid it while he was in a hurry to leave," Willow said, and continued reading.

The story goes that the Rebels took it after ambushing and killing everyone. I don't think so. Best I remember after all these months, this is what he said:

"Here she says she doesn't believe the official account of what happened. Now listen carefully to each word, because here's the clue that Ben wanted Edna to catch."

You and the baby are the rock foundation of my life. Wherever I travel on the road of life, I will treasure you. I hope to return, but if I don't, I want you to find comfort in the richness of our love.

"We already talked about the words, treasure and richness, that might refer to the money. I'm sure that they do. But we ignored some other key words, like 'rock foundation' and 'road of life.' "

Hugh was smiling and nodding agreement. Maggie and Mitch both stood up at the same time. Maggie started to say something, but Jerry pulled on her blouse. He shook his head and cocked it toward Willow. Maggie closed her mouth.

Willow was glorying in her leadership. For once her family was interested in her for something other than

And Tyler, Too?

getting her a husband. She could tell from the glances of most of the adults that they were beginning to understand where the money was. Since the children didn't, she explained. "You see, kids, I think when Grandpa Ben said 'road of life' that he meant this road that goes right by here. Back in his day, this was an important road from town toward St. Louis. And when he said 'rock foundation,' I think he meant this rock glade right here."

She stepped up on the undercut end of the biggest rock. It moved slightly under her weight. "When I looked out the cabin door after the storm, the first thing I saw was this solid rock right smack in the middle of the road. Hugh and I almost lost our lives in the river, and we might have been struck by that big oak tree. But it fell the other direction. So Grandpa Ben's words made sense. This was the 'rock foundation' on the 'road of life' which would lead to 'richness and comfort.' I think that he and his men pried up this slab and put the bags of money under it."

"But how could they have moved the rock?" Charley asked. He walked around it. "That slab is over eight feet wide and probably a foot thick."

Now that Willow had said what she wanted, she let the others figure out the logistics. Maggie and Mitch were excited. The children ran to join Willow on the rock, jumping up and down to make it totter more. The brothers and Jerry were thinking.

"We don't know how many men Ben had," Jerry said, moving over to the rock, "but he must have had seven or eight, and that many men could have pried up this slab, especially using their horses to pull it up."

"And when it was up far enough, they could have put logs or rails in as props to hold it in place," Mitch said, sending Willow a congratulatory glance.

Charley joined those at the slab. "Then they could have hollowed out a place to put the bags. . . ."

"And let the rock fall back," Gene said.

"Right here in front of them all the time," Charley's wife said.

"And no one ever suspected," Amy added.

"Until Aunt Willow figured it all out," Cory said, holding her hand.

Dawn had Willow's other hand. Jerry and Mitch were patting her on the back. The others were circled around her. Of all the excited people, only Hugh remained seated, smiling, an observer of the descendants of Ben and Edna Dawson gathered around Willow.

"You've solved it!" Cory and Dawn said over and over.

"All this is well and good," Jerry said, "as a theory. But that's what it is, a theory. A better one, I'd say, than any others so far—like Fall-in-Bluff." He grinned at Maggie. "But still a theory." He took off his hat and scratched his head. He looked at the slab. "Willow, you may be right. Let's see if it's so." He, as all the others, now knew the purpose of the things Willow had asked them to bring.

Charley studied the site, and ignoring much advice where to put his wrecker, backed it to the edge of the big slab. He lowered the cable from his crane and hooked it over the washed-out edge. Mitch led the other men to his truck for the crowbars, jacks, chains, heavy metal rods, shovels, mattocks, and trowels that Willow had put on his list to bring.

It took several attempts to get the cable and hook to catch onto the lip of the limestone slab because it kept slipping and breaking off pieces of rock. Gene, Mitch, Jerry, and Hugh each with a crowbar thrust under the slab raised it enough that Willow and Amy could slip a chain under an angled corner of the slab. They fastened both ends of the looped chain to the wrecker hook.

"Stand back!" Jerry yelled at the women and children gathered around. The children's mothers pulled them back toward the fallen oak. To the three men straining against their crowbars to hold the slab in mid-air, Jerry cautioned, "As soon as the crane takes hold, get back." They all nodded.

"Okay, Charley," Willow yelled. "Easy. Just a few feet."

Charley was looking out his back window, watching Willow for directions. From his seat he couldn't see the hook. Willow held her right hand in the air. With her left she motioned for him to operate the crane. Carefully he raised the cable until the hook took all the slack from the chain. Willow motioned him on. The crane lifted the rock a few inches. The men thrust their crowbars farther under it. When Charley tried to raise the slab more, the front wheels of the light wrecker left the ground. Willow motioned him to stop.

She and Amy pushed some of the shorter iron rods in to hold the slab where it was. Charley came back to look over the situation. "Have to pull forward. The truck's too light."

He returned to the cab and eased forward. At first the back wheels spun on the loose gravel, but then when he moved forward a few inches to solid rock, the tires had enough traction. Slowly the end of the rock slab raised. The men dropped their crowbars and stepped back out of the way in case the slab should break or fall. Willow kept motioning Charley to inch forward. When her end of the slab was about three feet off the ground, she had him stop. "Far enough," she yelled.

The men propped the slab with several rods. Then they gathered to decide what to do. Charley was for pulling the slab completely off. The others vetoed that. There would be a huge hole to fill. With the slab gone, the aesthetics of the rocky glade would be ruined. No one wanted that.

Jerry was examining the slab. It varied in thickness from eighteen inches to two feet with no visible crevices or faults to indicate that it might break. He said, "Charley, if you can raise the end another foot, that should be enough to get in to check for the money." As it was, there wasn't enough space for an adult to crawl in.

"I can get in there," Dawn said.

"Yeah, Dawn and me can," Cory said.

Both children ran from their mothers and started to crawl in. Jerry caught Cory with his overall straps. Willow grabbed Dawn's leg as she was on her hands and knees almost inside.

"Not so fast, kiddos," Jerry said. "The rock might fall on you."

"And mash you like a bug," Gene said, picking up Dawn and setting her beside her mother. Both children stayed back.

"I'm not too sure of raising it any higher, Dad," Charley said, "if you want to save the rock." He walked around the slab, pressing on it with his hand and tentatively testing it with his heavy boots. It didn't move. Then he checked his chain. "The weakest part is the chain. Let's put another chain around it."

Gene and Mitch were already stretching a chain on the ground in front of the gaping rock. One on each end, they pulled it under the slab. Charley was standing on top of the slab beside the cable and hook from his crane. He fastened the ends of the new chain together and hooked them to another longer chain which he wrapped around a hickory tree. Now both the wrecker crane and the tree were holding the slab in the air at a forty-five-degree angle.

"That should do it," he said. "If Ben Dawson did it with men and horses, we should be able to do it with my wrecker." To prove it, he jumped up and down on the raised slab. Mitch and Gene joined him. The chains didn't give. The slab was secure, held from above and propped underneath with the iron bars.

"Let me crawl in first," Willow said. "Next to the kids, I'm the smallest one here."

"Except Barney." Cory laughed because the collie was already inside, sniffing around.

The three-foot opening allowed her to crawl on her hands and knees for only a few inches. The slant of the slab and its increased thickness as she crawled farther made it necessary for her to stretch out on her stomach. Carefully avoiding the props, she wormed her way back using her elbows. As she moved, she felt around with her hands for any indication of something buried.

"It wouldn't be that far back," Mitch said. "Wouldn't Ben bury it nearer the edge?"

"But we don't know that he pried the slab up from the same side that we did," Willow answered.

After covering all the area she could with no success, she backed out. Hugh and Mitch were digging along the edges with shovels and mattocks. In some places they struck solid rock. The soil they found was dry and loose, easy to dig.

"I bet he put the bags in one of these dirt pockets near the edge," Mitch said. "But which edge?"

"Willow," Hugh said quietly so that the others didn't hear him. "Here." He pointed with his shovel to a shallow pocket about three feet from the edge.

Willow crawled in on her stomach in two feet of space. With a trowel, she scraped the fine dirt aside. Under a three-inch layer, her trowel struck something that gave when she pushed it, like large pieces of gravel. She grinned and looked at Hugh. She nodded her head. "There's something here."

Discarding her trowel, she dug with both hands, like a beaver digging a hole in the river bank.

"What've you found?"

"Is it the gold, Aunt Willow?"

"Be careful, dear."

There was a beam of light from a flashlight. She looked up to see Hugh squatting just inside the opening, holding the light at her flying hands. The squatting or prone forms of everyone in her family were ringed around the raised slab. Hardly daring to breathe, they watched her. The afternoon sun did not penetrate back where she was so that even the flashlight didn't show them her hands.

She pulled out one of the gravel-like objects. And that's what it was—gravel. Disappointed, she dug

And Tyler, Too?

deeper. Her fingers found more objects—round and flat and smooth. Though she and Mitch often used to find rocks in that shape that would skim across the river when they threw them, she knew this was no rock. She held it up in the beam of light.

All could see that it was an old gold coin.

Chapter Fourteen

In New York City a few weeks later, Willow hurried down Fifth Avenue from Grand Central Station to her office building. The morning was still cool. As usual, the morning rush of traffic and pedestrians excited her. Adjusting her shoulder tote pack filled with everything she needed, including her heels, she tried to keep her mind on her plans for the day that she'd finalized on her forty-five-minute train ride from her apartment in Tarrytown, but the rush of other men and women like her hurrying to work distracted her.

She stopped by one of Lord & Taylor's window displays out of the stream of people. Even after eight years she could hardly believe she was part of this scene, hurrying down Fifth Avenue daily on her ten-minute hike from the station. She blended in with the other businesswomen as she stepped quickly along in her sneakers. Her printed sarong skirt and matching print tank top with loose solid-colored jacket was becoming to her slim figure. Her newly styled hairdo framed her rosy face that still showed tan from the Missouri sun, but her hands grasping her laptop computer showed little evidence of their recent manual labor. Though the nails had not grown back to their normal tapered length, they were manicured and polished.

She loved being a part of the city. She hugged the knowledge that she would probably be made a vice-president. Creating an exclusive line of boys' clothing for Save-Mart stores was quite a coup. Mansfield & Logan usually supplied department stores and small shops. She was breaking new ground for her company by opening the door into the mass market while still retaining their quality and uniqueness. Her new line brought in an initial two-million-dollar order. And that was only the beginning. A whole new avenue of markets would undoubtedly follow.

Paula, one of her designers who kept up on all the gossip, had hinted of the promotion when she returned from the Ozarks. Getting the Save-Mart order almost ensured it. Willow entered her building at the 34th Street doors and rode the crowded elevator to the fifteenth floor. A quick stop in the ladies' room to change shoes, comb her hair, check on her makeup, and put on some dangling earrings, and she was ready for a busy day. In her office two designers were waiting for her; she had three calls to return, and an interview scheduled with a prospective assistant. She had a pile of mail and papers on her desk to go through, and her boss wanted to see her when she had a minute. With a happy sigh, she delved into her day's work.

Three hours later, caught up and exhilarated, she took a brief break for coffee. She leaned back in her swivel chair, kicked off her heels, and gave her tiny office a satisfied scan. Again she sighed happily. She could hardly contain herself. Her boss had confirmed her promotion, she just hired a promising-appearing assistant, and . . .

The receptionist entered with a couple of sheets from the main office fax machine. The notes were from Mitch. Willow smiled. Seeing Mitch's scrawled signature sent her thoughts back to the Ozarks. Since her return, she sometimes had difficulty keeping the thoughts of her experiences there from interfering with her work. When she glanced up from her computer out her window to rest her eyes, she saw trees and rivers instead of the canyon of tall buildings with streams of cars and humanity at its base. While working with Paula at the design computer, instead of seeing the clothing designs before her, she saw Hugh's sketches. But trained to discipline her interests into separate time slots, this morning she had been able to blot out those delightful thoughts and focus on her work. The break and Mitch's message gave her the excuse she needed to think about her family, about the discovery of the Union payroll, the cabin, and the new family corporation. And about Hugh.

She had a good excuse because Mitch's note began with news of Hugh. *Tyler has the windows and doors in. You should see what a difference the windows make in the appearance of the cabin. It no longer looks like a blind beggar. He shored up the west end that sagged by repairing the foundation. He cleaned the flue so that it's safe to use the fireplace. Everything looks great. I haven't seen much of him, as he's been drawing and painting like mad.*

Willow smiled. Since that impassioned good-bye kiss at the airport, she hadn't heard from him directly,

And Tyler, Too? 175

though Mitch and her mother kept her notified about his actions.

She continued reading Mitch's note. *Good news, Gene says that the gold is ours. The government has no claim on it. He's getting the coins appraised now, but we still don't know what they are worth. He's setting up an account and working on the papers for a not-for-profit corporation. I'm in his office now. While I'm here with him, fax me back right away your vote for officers. Also check over these tentative goals and bylaws for the corporation.*

Willow read over the bylaws and after making a few minor corrections, faxed them and her choice of officers back. She added a P.S. *Tell Mom I'm now a vice-president of Mansfield & Logan.*

Mitch's answer came back within ten minutes: *Gene and I approve of your corrections to the bylaws. And it seems everyone but me voted the same way. So here's the slate: President, Mitch Willard; First Vice-president, Willow Hill; Second Vice-president, Charley Hill; Secretary, Maggie Hill; Treasurer, Gene Hill. Board of directors and voting members, Mitch, Maggie, Willow, Gene, Charley; junior board, Cory and Dawn. We'll soon be in business. Gene will send you the papers to sign and your stock certificates. Congratulations on your promotion. We're proud of you and we miss you.*

Back in her skyscraper office, her rural vacation seemed like a fairy tale to her. Even while she was living it, it lacked reality. Now in retrospect, it was even more unbelievable. The three weeks home seemed more like a dream than real. Finding long-lost treasure was pure fantasy. Things like that didn't happen in the real world. Yet it had occurred right there on the Hill family's rocky glade. Falling in love in the midst of a tornado on a float trip was just romantic tripe. That, too, happened.

Then she scolded herself. What on earth possessed her to say that? Fallen in love? She didn't know. She liked Hugh, his talent, his gentleness, his understanding, his lips against hers, and his arms around her. She pictured him when she boarded the plane in Springfield. After his long kiss—she admitted she kissed back—he watched her walk out to the small plane that would take her to the St. Louis airport. At the door, she turned to wave. Standing in the glassed-in waiting room, he waved back with both arms over his head. From her window seat, she watched him. He did not leave. When the plane turned and taxied down the runway for takeoff, she waved one last time. From her distance it looked to her like he threw her a kiss.

How did she feel about him? Love? She didn't know then or now. Since then his only communication was a sketch he asked Mitch to fax to her. She pulled it out from under her blotter to look at it again for the umpteenth time. The scene was an aerial view from the back of the cabin. This angle showed a panorama. In the foreground bending over the cabin were the huge oak and walnut trees. The bluff, bottom fields, and the river were visible in the background. But the focus of the drawing was the open glade where ten people and a dog circled another figure who was holding something in her hands. Though done with few strokes, each person was recognizable—Willow and each member of her family. Standing apart from the

And Tyler, Too? 177

rest was a man whose only recognizable feature was long hair.

These words were written in the cloudless sky: *And Tyler, too?* Its message was clear. Hugh wanted to be a part of the family. If ever a picture was worth more than a thousand words, this was it.

Mitch's faxes and her parents' phone calls kept Willow apprised of Hugh's activities. He was thoroughly enjoying camping out at the cabin. Besides the improvements to the cabin itself, he repaired the damage done to the rock road from lifting the big slab. He hauled in enough gravel and dirt to smooth the surface. "The rock doesn't move when you step on it anymore," her father had told her in one of their long telephone conversations, "and Tyler has leveled it off so that we can drive right over it again like we used to. No one would ever know that it once covered up all that money."

"And he sawed up that old oak tree that the storm blew down," Maggie said. "He rolled a big block of the trunk off to the side to make a place to sit and look over the bluff."

"And, Willow," her father said, "you ought to see the stack of firewood piled up to use in the fireplace—"

Maggie kept interrupting. "I don't know how he found the time to do it, but he cut a cross-section chunk from the thickest part of the trunk to make a picnic table."

"Yeah, he said since he sort of ruined the rock slab for eating, we needed another place."

Willow was filled in on what Hugh was doing, though not what he was thinking. She wished she were two people. She loved it here, but she felt left out of the things happening at home. It seemed to her now that she was the lone figure standing outside the family circle while Hugh was inside. However, she quickly banished the fleeting thought that she could move back there if she wanted to. No way would she leave what she had here.

Then she wondered if Hugh would stay in the Ozarks. He appeared to love it there. He could stay. Frequent trips to confer with his customers was all the time he needed to be in the city. But she doubted he wanted to leave New York. Being there was like an assignment. He even admitted to her that he was doing research. His enthusiasm was in part because of his use of the Ozarks in his career. Merely temporary.

She glanced once again at his sketch. Just before she slipped it back under the blotter, she reread his question. *And Tyler, too?* She smiled with pleasure when she thought of the possibilities behind that question and how she might answer him.

Willow became aware that Paula was standing at her office door. Paula was grinning with the same expression she had when Willow first returned from her vacation—an I-know-something-you-don't-know-I-know expression. Willow hadn't planned to say anything at the office about Hugh's being with her, but they already knew. The garment industry was like a small community in the big city. Hugh had told a friend and soon everyone knew. Willow's family were not the only ones interested in her single status. Without her knowing it they had tagged her as eligible bachelorette number one.

Since Paula already knew, Willow had to tell her a

little more about her vacation with Tyler. At the office she reverted to using his last name. Her expressions and the eagerness in her voice were too revealing for Paula not to catch on how successful the visit had been. So when Paula appeared at her door with this same grin on her face, Willow wondered what new pieces of gossip she had heard.

"You have a visitor," was all that Paula said as she cocked her head down the hall toward the conference room.

"Okay, be there in a minute." Willow finished the now-lukewarm coffee and pushed the mug from the edge of her desk. "Just more business," she reasoned. Slipping her heels back on, she started down the hall. Another designer grinned at her as she passed the design room. At the sample room door, a couple of the Puerto Rican pattern makers smiled at her.

She met her boss in the narrow hall. He also wore the same crazy grin everyone had. "This seems to be your day, Willow." He cocked his head toward the conference room and repeated Paula's words, "You have a visitor."

She stepped into the room expecting to see a prospective buyer or one of the many salesmen who came regularly. Standing with his back to the door while he looked out the window was a medium-sized man dressed completely in layered black clothes with his black hair almost hiding his collar. Willow's heart skipped a beat even before he turned around. "Hi, Tippy," Hugh said, his head slightly bent and tilted to the side as he looked at her. His face was tanner than before and he was growing a beard. He had never looked more handsome. "I'm back."

Seeing him again in New York garb almost shocked her. She had become used to him in Missouri in T-shirts and jeans or shorts. She'd almost forgotten his artist persona. Then she realized that to him she also looked quite different in her stylish outfit and bold jewelry, instead of shorts and sloppy shirts.

"Hugh," she said. They both stepped together in a hug which turned into a long kiss. Hugh held her face between his hands as he studied it. "Hi," he said again. He grinned. She ran her hand over his beard that almost covered the cleft in his chin.

"Like it?" he asked. "Too much trouble to shave in the wilderness, so I let it grow. I thought I'd see if you think I should shave it off."

Willow stood back at arm's length to study him. "It looks good. Makes you look distinguished."

"Ugh! That'll never do." He shuddered in mock exaggeration at ruining his artsy appearance.

"But I like you better without it. It hides your dimple." She traced the cleft with her finger.

"Me, too," Hugh said. He stared at her as if he couldn't see enough. He brushed the back of his hand over her cheek and kissed her again.

"Congratulations. I hear you're vice-president."

"How did you . . . ?" Then she turned around to see Paula and some other colleagues enjoying the scene from the open door. "She told you?" When Hugh nodded, Willow laughed. "I guess New York is no different from home after all."

"No, not really." He grinned at the women. "Same objectives, just different people, different scenery. Both good places."

"Yes, they are. I thought you might want to stay there."

Hugh laughed. "No. It wasn't nearly as much fun after you left. No floods or storms. Not even a farm auction or a glimpse of an otter." He played with her dangling earring as he watched her face. "Just work."

"Did you get much done?"

"I never worked so hard. I've got several sketch pads full and rolls of photographs. Enough to last me for months. Good stuff. Good enough that..." He pulled her down to a chair and sat beside her. "And, Willow, you aren't the only one with good news. I just came from an editor friend of mine. I showed him a few drawings. He likes them, and he's going to pitch my book idea of a series of paintings to his publisher. There's a good chance they'll give me a contract."

"Oh, how wonderful." She ran her fingers over his beard, her eyes dancing with mischief. "So your research trip into the Ozarks and native family life there was successful?"

"That mission accomplished. But I'm not sure about my main objective."

Willow ignored his last comment. "I liked the sketch you faxed me."

"I hoped you would."

"It pretty much says everything, doesn't it?"

"I thought so. Beautiful place, family togetherness, enjoying their poetic and literal richness, and an outsider's loneliness. Do you have an answer to the question I jotted on it?"

Willow was conscious of the women who were still watching them. "Was there a question?" she teased him.

"You know very well there was. The one the outsider was asking as he watched the close-knit group."

"And Tyler, too?"

Hugh nodded eagerly. "That's the one."

She lowered her eyebrows in serious contemplation. "I've thought a long time about that."

"You have?" He cocked his slightly bent head and looked up at her.

"Yes." Willow then grinned at him, and taking his hand, pulled him up and dragged him to the hall door. "And I think that the one member of the Hill family who is now also out of the family circle, should not let Tyler stand all by himself. So she should invite him to join her for lunch." She grinned at the women who had to step back to let them pass. "Then he won't be lonely anymore."

"Just for lunch?" he asked, turning her around to face him. "What about for the rest of our lives?"

Her heart lurched at his strong touch and the seriousness in his eyes. Behind him she could see the interested faces of the women who were watching them closely—just like her family did on her vacation. Instead of the serious answer she wanted to make, she said lightly for the benefit of the audience, "That could be arranged."

Blushing, feeling awkward, but laughing, she pulled him down the hall to the main door of her company's suite of offices. Just before Hugh closed behind them the glass-fronted door with the lettering *Mansfield & Logan, Inc.,* he faced Paula and the other women, grinned, and gave them an exaggerated thumbs-up sign.

"I saw that," Willow said, but she lifted her laughing face to him and kissed him quickly on his lips. They ran to reach the elevators just before the door closed on one going down.